THE *BUSY* BODY

DONALD E. WESTLAKE

MYSTERIOUSPRESS.COM

OPEN ROAD

INTEGRATED MEDIA

NEW YORK

Copyright © 1966 by Donald E. Westlake

ISBN: 978-1-5040-6810-9

This edition published in 2021 by MysteriousPress.com/Open Road Integrated Media, Inc.
180 Maiden Lane
New York, NY 10038
www.openroadmedia.com

To Henry *and* Nedra

THE *BUSY* BODY

If anyone shall dig up and plunder a buried corpse he shall be outlawed until he comes to an agreement with the relatives of the dead man, and they ask that he be allowed to come among men again.

The Salic Law, c. 490

Anything awful makes me laugh. I misbehaved once at a funeral.

Charles Lamb

1

ENGEL'S KNEES HURT. THIS was the first time he'd been inside a church in twelve years, and he wasn't used to it any more. He'd come in here, all unknowing, and the first thing he knew he was on his knees on this hard wooden plank, and pretty soon the kneecaps had started burning, and then shooting pains had developed up and down the legs, and by now he was almost sure something was broken down there and he'd never walk again.

To his left, blocking the aisle directly in front of the altar, was Charlie Brody's casket, draped with a black cloth bearing a gold embroidered cross. It was really very fancy-looking, and a nutty rhyme began to circulate around in Engel's head: A tisket, a tasket,/A black and yellow basket,/Charlie Brody kicked the bucket/And now he's in a casket,/A casket,/And now he's in a casket.

The rhyme struck him funny, and he grinned a little, but then out of the corner of his eye he saw Nick Rovito giving him the fish-eye, so he dummied up again. Then his left knee suddenly gave him a particularly vicious twinge, and he got on his face an expression Nick Rovito couldn't possibly object to. He leaned as much weight as possible on his forearms resting on the back of the pew in front of him, and he wondered how much longer this foofaraw was going to take.

In a way, none of this was even necessary, since Charlie Brody hadn't kicked off in the line of duty, hadn't been gunned down or anything like that. All he'd had was a heart attack. Of course, he'd had it just when he was putting some water on to boil for instant coffee, and he'd fallen over with his head in the flame, so he was just as much a mess now as if he *had* been rubbed out—closed coffin and all, no viewing the remains, the whole bit—but nevertheless, in the old days this sort of big-shot funeral had been reserved either for VIPs or guys sliced down on the job.

It was because of the New Look, that's what it was. With the New Look, practically nobody ever got rubbed out any more, not so's the body was left around, not since Anastasia, and that was just some guys showing off. With the New Look, there weren't any rival organizations to have gang wars with, because the Central Committee gave everybody a territory and then settled all jurisdictional disputes itself at the conference table down in Miami. And with the New Look, nobody shot it out with the cops any more, they just went along nice and quiet and let the organization lawyers handle everything. So, because of the New Look, it had been years and years since the organization had been able to throw a really first-class supercolossal Cecil B. DeMille extravaganza of a funeral.

And now here was Charlie Brody, not much more than a punk. A courier is all he was, between the organization here in New York and the suppliers down in Baltimore. But he was dead, and he was the first active member of the organization to kick off in three or four years, and when Nick Rovito heard about it he'd rubbed his hands together and got a gleam in his eye and said, "Let's us give old Charlie Brody a *send*-off! What I mean, a send-off!"

The other guys around the table had all looked pleased and said sure, good old Charlie Brody, the guy deserved a good send-off, but it was obvious they hadn't been thinking about good old Charlie Brody at all, they'd been thinking about the send-off.

Engel was still pretty new at these meetings, so he hadn't said much of anything, but he too had been pleased at the idea. He'd joined the organization too late to have any memories of send-offs himself, but he could remember his father talking about them when he was a kid. "That was a *grand* send-off," his father used to say. "The church packed to the rafters, five thousand people on the sidewalks outside, mounted cops all over the place. The Mayor showed up, and the Sanitation Commissioner, and everybody. That was a *great* send-off!"

Not that Engel's father had ever been high enough in the organization to rate a seat at a send-off like that, but more than once he'd been a part of that crowd of five thousand on the outside. At his own funeral, three years ago, there'd been only twenty-seven people. None of the bigwigs in the organization had shown up except Ludwig Meyershoot, who'd been Engel's father's boss for eighteen years.

But now, nostalgia in their eyes, the boys were deciding to give the recent Charlie Brody a grand-slam all-stops-out good old-fashioned send-off. Nick Rovito rubbed his hands together and said, "Somebody call Saint Pat's."

Somebody else at the table said, "Nick, I don't think Charlie was Catholic."

Nick Rovito looked indignant and said, "Who cares what the hell Charlie was? No church on earth can give you a send-off like the Catholic Church. Whadaya want, a bunch a *Quakers* sitting around, looking gloomy, spoiling the whole occasion?"

Nobody had wanted that, so Charlie was getting a good Catholic send-off, with Latin lyrics and sharp costuming and good strong incense and a lot of holy water and the whole complete routine. It wasn't Saint Pat's, that had already been reserved, but it was a church over in Brooklyn, almost as big, and nearer the cemetery anyway.

Only if he'd remembered about the knees, Engel told himself, he would of come down with a virus this morning and let somebody else play pallbearer, the hell with it.

Well. The service was anyway grinding to a close. Nick Rovito got to his feet, and the other five pallbearers got to their feet right after him. Engel's knees cracked so loud you could hear an echo bounce back off the stone wall of the church. Nick Rovito gave him the fish-eye again, but what could Engel do? He couldn't stop his knees from cracking, could he?

His legs were so stiff he was afraid for a second he wouldn't be able to walk. They were all over pins and needles, like there hadn't been any blood getting down there in quite a while. He flexed them, doing half a deep-knee bend before he realized he was in the front row of the church practically and everybody could see him, so he straightened quick and went on out to the aisle with the others.

His place was at the left rear. They all stood there in position a second, their backs to the altar, and Engel could see all the people jammed into the church. Not counting the undercover FBI agents and the undercover Crime Commission agents and the undercover Treasury agents and the undercover Narcotics Squad agents, and not counting the newspaper reporters and the wire service reporters and the photographers and the lady reporters to write the human interest stories, there were still maybe four hundred people in the church that had been invited by Nick Rovito.

The Mayor wasn't there, but he'd sent the Housing Commissioner in his place. Besides him there were three Congressmen that had come up through the ranks and gone on to represent the organization down in Washington, and a few singers and comics that were owned by the organization and fronted night clubs and restaurants for the organization, and a lot of lawyers in very conservative suits, and a few doctors looking fat and dyspeptic the way doctors do, and some sympathetic-looking people from the Department of Health, Education & Welfare, and some television and advertising executives that hadn't known Charlie Brody at all but did know Nick Rovito socially, and a lot of other notables. It was a very distinguished crowd, all in all, and Charlie Brody would have been flabbergasted if he could have seen them.

Nick Rovito, at the front right slot, nodded his head in the signal, and Engel and the other pallbearers bent and fumbled under the black drape for the coffin handles, and then straightened and lifted the coffin up onto their shoulders. One of the ushers quick wheeled the coffin rack out of the way so it wouldn't show in the news pictures, and then the pallbearers started down the aisle with flashbulbs popping all over the place. Engel was the tallest pallbearer, so he was the one carrying most of the weight; with the coffin grinding down onto his shoulder, he was forgetting all about his knees.

They marched on down the aisle, in slow time, with the faces on both sides looking solemn and serious, thinking about life and death and eternity and would some damn fool of a photographer take their picture by mistake even after the warning Nick Rovito had given the newspapers, and then they marched out into the sunlight and down the long shallow steps toward the hearse.

It was really quite a sight. The sidewalk was roped off on both sides, and just inside the ropes there were cops standing around with white helmets reflecting the sun, and back of the ropes there was a sea of people in Hawaiian shirts and Bermuda shorts. It all made Engel think of fruit juice, and that reminded him he was thirsty, and that reminded him he was dying for a smoke. Well. Later.

He knew his mother was down in the mob somewhere, and he knew she was probably jumping up and down and waving the *Daily News* to try to attract his attention, so after the first quick glance at the mob he kept his eyes straight ahead, staring at the hearse. He was feeling a little stage fright anyway, out there in front of all those people, and if he should happen to see his mother jumping up and down and waving a newspaper at him besides, it would be too much. He knew his mother was proud of him for making it so much bigger than his father, who until the day of his death was never more than a store-front bookie and game operator in Washington Heights, but later on would be time enough to look at her and listen to her praises.

He and the others marched across the sidewalk now to where the undertaker was standing beside the hearse. The undertaker was so tanned he looked like he'd been covered with bronze paint. When Engel got closer, he saw it was paint, that stuff you can get in the drugstore to give yourself a fake tan. The way he could tell, the undertaker hadn't gotten it on even; up close, his face looked blotched and patchy, like he was a map of Europe done in shades of brown.

The undertaker was smiling so hard Engel was afraid he'd rip his cheeks. He kept motioning at the hearse like he wanted the pallbearers and everybody to just climb right on in and they'd take a spin through Chinatown, but they didn't. There was a hydraulic slab covered with purple felt that swung out from the interior of the hearse, and this is what they set the coffin on. Then the driver of the hearse pushed a button on the dashboard and the hydraulic slab swung back in again, and the undertaker and one of his assistants shut the doors. The undertaker said to Nick Rovito, "It's going beautifully, wouldn't you say?"

But Nick Rovito wouldn't say anything during a send-off; a send-off was too solemn an occasion. Engel saw him give the undertaker the fish-eye, and then he saw the undertaker decide to keep his trap shut from now on.

Nick Rovito motioned, and he and the other pallbearers stood to one side for a minute. The hearse drove forward, down the cleared space along the curb, and one of the flower cars drove up behind it. There were three flower cars. Ushers began carrying flowers out of the church, and in just a few minutes all three flower cars were full up, and then the procession cars came along.

The procession cars were Nick Rovito's idea. They were all black Cadillac convertibles, with the tops down. "This is going to be a modren send-off," Nick had said. "Not just a great send-off, a *modren* send-off." One of the other guys at the table had said, "To symbolize the new era, huh, Nick?" and Nick Rovito had said, "Yeah."

Now the people started coming down out of the church, in twos, with Charlie Brody's widow and Archie Freihofer in the lead. Archie Freihofer ran the girl part of the operation. Since Charlie Brody hadn't left any insurance, and since his dying outside the line of duty meant his widow wouldn't be getting any pension from the organization, and since she was a fine-looking blonde even in basic black like today, she was going to go back to working for Archie again now, like she was before she married Charlie, so it was only right that Archie should escort her at the send-off.

The undertaker had a little notebook where he'd written down who was going to go in what car, and now he read off, "Car number one, Mrs. Brody, Mr. Freihofer, Mr. Rovito, Mr. Engel."

Nick Rovito got into the back seat first, and then Charlie's widow, and then Archie Freihofer. Engel got in front next to the driver, and the convertible slid forward to close the gap with the flower car in front, and the other four pallbearers got into the second car.

For the next fifteen minutes it was stop and go, stop and go, while back there in front of the church the convertibles got filled, one after the other. There were thirty-four of them, which was Nick Rovito's idea. "One for every year of Charlie's life," he'd said. Somebody else at the table had said, "That's real poetic, Nick," and Nick Rovito had said, "Yeah."

Everybody was silent now for a while. It was hot out here in the sun with the top down. Engel smoked a cigarette, not looking to see if Nick Rovito wanted to give him the fish-eye or not, and he watched the people on the sidewalk point out Nick Rovito to their kids. "That's Nick Rovito, the big gangster," they told their kids. "He's got millions of dollars, and beautiful women, and imported booze, and influence in high places. He's a very evil man and I don't want you to grow up like that. See him in the fancy car there?"

Nick Rovito just kept looking straight ahead. Most times he'd wave to kids, and smile, and wink, but this was too solemn an occasion for that.

After a while Charlie's widow began to cry. "Charlie was a right guy," she said, crying. "We had seventeen beautiful months together."

"That's right, honey," said Archie Freihofer, and he patted her knee.

"I wish there could of been a viewing," she said. She dabbed at her eyes with a little handkerchief. "I wish I could of seen him one last time. I give them his good shoes and his French undies and his Brooks Brothers shirt and his Italian tie and his good blue suit, and they decked him all out, and nobody couldn't even see him to say a good-bye."

She was getting more and more broken up about it. Nick Rovito patted her other knee and said, "That's okay, Bobbi, it's better to remember him like he used to be."

"I guess you're right," she said.

"Sure I am. You got him all decked out, huh? Blue suit and everything. Which blue suit was that?"

"He only had one blue suit," she said.

"The one he traveled in."

"Every time he come home, that's what he was wearing." The thought broke her up all over again, and she went back to crying.

"There, there," said Archie Freihofer. He squeezed her knee this time.

Finally all the cars back there were full, and the procession got on the road. They drove over to the Belt Parkway and headed south. The speed limit was fifty miles an hour, but the church ceremony had run a little over, so they took Charlie to the cemetery at seventy miles an hour.

The cemetery was out by Paerdegat Basin, out back of a new housing development glistening in the sunlight over there like a lot of shiny new toys from Japan. Everybody got out of the cars, and the pallbearers got the coffin and carried it over to where the grave workers had the straps laid out. They put the coffin down on the straps, and then the priest made a speech in English, and the grave workers pressed a button that made the machinery around the straps buzz and lower the coffin into the hole, and then it was all over. Engel, now that he was out standing on grass, was thinking what a nice day it was for golf, and wondering if the municipal golf course would be too crowded by now. Probably would be. (His mother had made him get interested in golf, because she said it was the game executives played.)

On the way back to the cars, Nick Rovito came close to Engel and said, his voice low, "Mark where they planted him."

Engel looked around, marking it, and said, "How come?"

Nick Rovito said, "On account of tonight you're digging him up again."

2

ALOYSIUS EUGENE ENGEL WAS born in a hospital in Washington Heights in upper Manhattan twenty-nine years, four months and three days before Nick Rovito told him he was going to be a grave robber. In the intervening period he had been a lot of things, but never once had he been a grave robber.

Engel was the only son of Fred P. Engel and Frances (Maloney) Engel. His father ran a small store on St. Nicholas Avenue, where for a front he sold cigarettes and magazines while in the back there was a perpetual poker game and in another room two telephones on which bets were taken. Engel's father worked for the organization on straight salary, plus he could keep whatever profit he made off the cigarettes and magazines, which wasn't much. Engel's mother worked since before he was born at the Paris Style Beauty Shoppe on 181st Street, where she was eventually the oldest and most valued employee. It had been her dream for years to start her own beauty shoppe, but Engel's father had the unhappy habit of placing bets with himself, trying to beat himself with the nags even though under his bookie hat he knew *nobody* beats the nags. But hope springs eternal, and Engel grew up in a household permanently on the brink of financial chaos.

Also arguments. Money troubles cause arguments in the best of marriages, and Engel's parents didn't have the best of marriages. So they'd scream at each other—in those days Engel's father still did some screaming himself, and occasional punching—and either Engel's mother or some neighbor woman was always calling the cops, until somebody had to come down from the organization headquarters and point out it was an embarrassment to the organization to have the cops forever coming by the apartment of one of the organization bookies, and after that the arguments were quieter because Engel's father stopped answering back.

It was probably his father's silence more than anything else that made Engel ultimately side with him. He knew, just as his father knew, that everything his mother hollered was true, but that wasn't the point. The point was, nobody's perfect, and if Engel's father's imperfection happened to be throwing his money away on a lot of gluepots, it could have been worse, so why not have a little understanding? By the time Engel was in high school, he was full to the brim with understanding for his father and silent rebellion against his mother.

So when his mother told him that after high school he should go on to college to make something of himself, "Not be a bum all your life like your old man, the bum," Engel resolutely turned his back. He got his high school diploma, went to his father, and said, "Introduce me to somebody, Dad. I want to go to work for the organization."

"Your mother wants you to go to college."

"I know."

Father and son looked at one another, and understood one another, and smiled at one another through their tears.

"Okay, son," said Engel's father. "I'll call Mr. Meyershoot downtown tomorrow."

So at seventeen Engel went to work for the organization, first as a messenger boy for Mr. Meyershoot, who had an office way downtown on Varick Street, and then later on in various capacities, including even strong-arm now and then even though he was only of moderate weight and not particularly mean of disposition. He had also once or twice been a union official, and he'd for a while been a courier something like the job Charlie Brody'd had, and he'd worked here and there in the organization. He moved from job to job more than the average, but that was because he was young and restless and always interested in new things.

Meanwhile his mother took about four years to get used to it. She blamed his father for being a bad influence, and gave him several million words on the subject, but eventually, in just about four years, she adapted herself to reality and stopped bugging him about missed opportunities.

On the other hand, once she adapted she had something new to say. "Make a name for yourself, Aloysius," she'd say. "Don't be like your bum of an old man, the bum, a regular stick in the mud, never moved up out of that crummy store in thirty-four years. Make your mark, move ahead in the world. If it's the organization you want to work for, *work* for it. Get *ahead*. After all, didn't Nick Rovito start at the bottom of the ladder, too?"

This kind of talk didn't bother him so much. He didn't possess much of the kind of ambition she was talking about—she wouldn't have liked to hear *how* Nick Rovito had come up from the bottom of the ladder, but Engel was never so unfair

17

as to tell her—but he was older now and able to let her words pass over him without leaving any marks. "Sure, Mom," he said sometimes, and other times he didn't say anything.

If it hadn't been for the Conelly blitzkrieg, Engel might have kept drifting along in the organization for years. But the Conelly blitzkrieg came along, and Engel was in the right place at the right time, and all of a sudden the kind of future his mother had been talking about for years was dumped in his lap. As his mother pointed out, all he had to do now was take the good things that were being offered him. He had it made.

The way the Conelly blitzkrieg happened to help Engel was a little complicated. Conelly was a big florid hearty happy guy, Nick Rovito's right hand. He and Nick Rovito had been partners for years, Conelly always at Nick Rovito's right hand. But something had happened to Conelly, something had suddenly made him too ambitious. Despite the Central Committee down in Miami, despite his years of friendship with Nick Rovito, despite the risk involved and the unlikelihood of success, Conelly decided to get rid of Nick Rovito and take over the organization himself.

Conelly wasn't working alone. He had friends in the organization, middle-range executives that were more loyal to Conelly than to Nick Rovito, and Conelly one by one brought them over to his side, planning and hoping for a bloodless palace revolution. One of the guys he brought over to his team was Ludwig Meyershoot, who was Engel's father's boss. And Ludwig Meyershoot, having a soft spot in his head for Fred Engel, tipped him to what was about to happen. "So you wouldn't wind up on the wrong side, Fred," he said.

Engel's father promptly told Engel's mother, who just as promptly said, "You know what *that* is, Fred Engel? *That* is your son's chance for advancement, high position, a life of luxury, all the things *you* never got."

Engel himself didn't know about any of this yet. He had his own place now, on Carmine Street in the Village, because of women. It always used to throw a damper on the proceedings when he would take a woman home for purposes of cohabitation and first have to introduce her to his mother. So now he had his own place and it worked out a lot better.

Meanwhile, uptown, Fred Engel was going through one of those conflicting loyalty problems that big dull serious novels are made on. He felt the loyalty of habit toward Ludwig Meyerhashoot. He felt the loyalty of awe toward Nick Rovito. And he felt the loyalty of blood toward his son.

Eventually the combination of Nick Rovito, blood ties and a shrill-voiced spouse did the trick. Fred Engel called his son to a meeting in the family apartment. "Al," he said, because no one on earth but his mother called Engel by his full first name of Aloysius, "Al, this is important. Conelly is going to try to take over from Nick Rovito. You know who I mean? You know Conelly?"

"I've seen him around," said Engel. "What do you mean, take over?"

"Take over," his father explained. "As in take over."

"You mean throw Nick Rovito out?"

"That's it."

"You sure? I mean, what I mean is, you sure?"

Engel's father nodded. "I got it from a unimpeachable source." he said. "But the thing is, I can't pass the word on to

Nick Rovito myself without lousing things up with my unimpeachable source, you know?"

Engel said, "So? How come?"

His father ignored the second part of that. In response to the first part he said, "So *you* tell him. I'll set things up so you can see him personally. Don't tell anybody but Nick Rovito himself, I don't know for sure who else is in it with Conelly."

Engel said, "Me? How come me?"

"Because there's nobody else," his father said. "And because," he said, and Engel's mother could be heard echoing in the words, "it can do you a lot of good in the organization."

Engel said, "I'm not sure . . ."

"Did I ever steer you wrong, Al?"

Engel shook his head. "No, you never did."

"And I won't this time."

"But what if Nick Rovito wants proof? I mean, what the hell, he don't know me from nobody, and Conelly's his right hand."

"Conelly's been dipping into the pension fund," his father told him. "He's been siphoning cash off into a secret account under Nick Rovito's name. That's the excuse he'll use with the Committee. I'll give you all the details I got, and when Nick Rovito says he wants proof you tell him what I'm telling you."

And that's what happened. Through guile, persistence, cunning and terror, Engel's father managed ultimately to arrange for the meeting between Engel and Nick Rovito, without having told Nick Rovito or anybody else what the meeting was for, and when Engel was alone with Nick Rovito and Nick Rovito's bodyguard he told everything his father had said, except he didn't say and wouldn't say where he got his information.

At first Nick Rovito refused to believe it. In fact, he got so irritated he grabbed Engel by the shirt front and bounced him up and down awhile for saying such things about his old friend Conelly. He had to reach up to do it, since Engel had about five inches and thirty pounds on him, but he could do it because Engel knew better than to defend himself. Still, despite the bouncing, Engel stuck to his story, not only because it was true but also because there was nothing else to do, and after a while Nick Rovito began to wonder, and then after a further while he sent somebody to go get Conelly "and tell him get his ass over here fast."

Conelly got there twenty minutes later, by which time Engel's shirt was wringing wet with perspiration. Nick Rovito said to Engel, "Tell Conelly what you told me."

Engel blinked. He cleared his throat. He scuffed his feet. He told Conelly what he'd told Nick Rovito.

When Engel was done, Nick Rovito said, "I haven't checked the kid's story yet, but I can. Do I have to?"

Conelly got purple in the face, said, "Gahhh!" and made a run for Engel, his hands out to take Engel apart.

Nick Rovito reached into a desk drawer, took out a gun and tossed it casually to Engel. It was the first time in his career Engel had even *held* a gun, but there was no time to think, what with Conelly and those hands getting rapidly closer, so Engel just closed his eyes and pulled the trigger five times, and when he opened his eyes again Conelly was lying on the floor.

Nick Rovito said to Engel, "You are my right hand, kid. From now on you're my right hand, with all that that implies."

"I think," said Engel, "I'm going to throw up."

And they both came to pass. Engel threw up, and became Nick Rovito's right hand, abruptly replacing Conelly at some whim of Nick Rovito's. This was four years ago, about a year before Engel's father died from gallstones and complications. For the last four years Engel had been Nick Rovito's right hand, which kind of meant private secretary, and all that that implied had been large amounts of money, new suits by the closetful, a far better class of woman, charge accounts in expensive restaurants, adoration from his mother (who now, through his financial help, had her own beauty shoppe), a key to the Playboy Club, instant obedience from the rank and file in the organization . . .

. . . and digging up bodies in cemeteries in the middle of the night.

3

SO THAT WAS IT for golf today, no question. Instead there was a meeting, right after the funeral.

The boys all sat around the table, looking at Nick Rovito because he'd called the meeting all of a sudden out there at the cemetery, and nobody knew what it was all about except Engel, and he didn't know much. Except there wasn't going to be any golf this afternoon for one thing, and for two things he was all of a sudden a body snatcher.

One of Archie's girls came into the room with ashtrays, spreading them around at all the places around the table, and Nick Rovito gave her the fish-eye and said, "You shoulda had the ashtrays out already. Memo pads, pencils, glasses, pitchers of water, ashtrays, all done before we got here."

"We didn't know nothing till the last minute," she said, and Nick Rovito said, "Shut up," and she shut up.

Everything else was already on the table at all the places. There were the little three-by-five memo pads and the long yellow sharpened pencils and the thick-bottomed water glasses and the fat pitchers each full of ice water. Archie's girl finished handing out the ashtrays and then she went away and shut the door.

Nick Rovito lit a cigar. It took him a long time. First he unwrapped it, and then he stuck the aluminum tube back in his pocket to give to his kid to make a rocket out of with match-heads, and then he smelled it, putting it up to his nose like a mustache, and then he looked contented a few seconds, and then he licked it all over to get it good and wet with saliva, and then he bit off the end and spat the shreds down on the carpet, and then he leaned forward a little and somebody stuck a hand out with a gas lighter in it going *hisssss*, and Nick Rovito lit his cigar. It had to be a gas lighter, not a lighter-fluid lighter, because Nick Rovito could taste the lighter fluid if he lit his cigar from a lighter-fluid lighter, so all the boys carried gas lighters, whether they smoked or not. You never knew when.

Nick Rovito took the cigar out of his mouth and watched the smoke a minute, coming up from the pale gray ash at the tip with the burning coal showing behind it, very luxurious, and the boys watched Nick Rovito watching the cigar smoke. Besides Engel, there were two others from the pallbearers, plus three guys that had been ushers. Everybody else from the funeral had gone home or gone to work, except the widow, who went off with Archie Freihofer.

"What I should a done," Nick Rovito told the cigar smoke, "what I should a done was not to waited. But I thought to myself, it's better to mind the amenidies, and wait till after the send-off, and then send somebody over to Charlie's old place and pick it up. What I didn't count on is a stupid broad who she isn't a brand-new widow I'd push her face in, that's what I didn't count on."

Somebody else around the table said, "Something wrong, Nick?"

Nick Rovito gave him the fish-eye and didn't answer him. Then he looked at Engel and said, "Tonight, Engel, sometime tonight you go dig him up, you got me?"

Engel nodded, but somebody else around the table said, "Dig him up? You mean, like Charlie? Dig him up?" and Nick Rovito said, "Yeah."

Somebody else around the table said, "How come, Nick?"

Nick Rovito made a disgusted face and said, "His suit. Charlie's blue suit, that's how come. That's what I want you to get me, Engel, the blue suit that dumb broad buried Charlie in."

Engel didn't get it for a second. He'd been thinking one way, and now it was some other way. He said, "You don't want the body?"

"Wha'd I want with a body? Don't talk stupid."

Somebody else around the table said, "What's so hot about this blue suit, Nick?"

Nick Rovito said, "Tell him, Fred."

Somebody else around the table—it was Fred Harwell, he'd been one of the pallbearers, too, Charlie'd worked direct for him—said, "Holy Jesus, Nick, you mean *the* blue suit?"

Nick Rovito nodded. "That's the one. Tell them about it."

"Holy Jesus," said Fred. But then he didn't say anything else. He acted stunned.

Nick Rovito told the story for him. "Charlie was a traveling man," he said. "He traveled for Fred here. He traveled to Baltimore, and then he traveled back to New York. On the train, so there's no reservations. Right, Fred?"

"Holy Jesus," said Fred. "*That* blue suit"

"That's the one." Nick Rovito puffed at his cigar and tapped some pale gray ash in the ashtray in front of him and said, "What Charlie did, he took things places. To Baltimore, he took money. From Baltimore back to New York, he brought horse, not yet cut. You got it now?"

Somebody around the table said, "In the suit? *In* it?"

"Sewed in the lining on the way down, the dough. Sewed in the lining on the way back, the horse. That suit was ripped up and sewed back together again once, twice a week for three years. You'd never *see* seams so good in a suit that old. Right, Fred?"

"Holy Jesus," said Fred. "I never thought."

"When Charlie kicked the bucket," Nick Rovito said, "he'd just come back from Baltimore. He had a couple hours before the drop, so he went home to make himself a cup of coffee, and the rest is history. Right, Fred?"

"It slipped my mind," said Fred. "It absolutely slipped my mind."

"A quarter of a million dollars' worth of heroin slipped your mind, Fred. And I knew it did, I knew you forgot all about it, and we got to talk about that sometime."

"Nick, I don't know why it happened, I swear to Christ I don't. I've had so much on my mind lately, this school rezoning's been driving me out of my mind, all of a sudden every kid on the payroll is all together at the same school and all the customers are to hell and gone the other side of Central Park, then there's been this rumor going around about airplane glue that's taking the customers away, and I—"

"We'll talk about that some other time, Fred. Right now the important thing is we get that suit back. Engel?"

Engel looked alert.

Nick Rovito said, "You got it, Engel? Tonight you dig him up and get me that suit."

Engel nodded. "I got it, Nick," he said.

Somebody around the table said, "Like Burke and Hare, huh, Nick?" and Nick Rovito said, "Yeah."

Engel said, "Yeah, come to think of it. Alone, Nick? That's a hell of a lot of digging. I need somebody to pitch in."

"So get somebody."

Somebody around the table said, "Hey! I got an idea, Nick."

Nick Rovito looked at him. Not the fish-eye, just blank, waiting.

The guy said, "I got this guy, this Willy Menchik. The one that fingered Gionno?"

Nick Rovito nodded. "I remember," he said.

"We got the clearance to rub him, just day before yesterday. I had it set up for over in Jersey, Friday night, he's on this bowling league, see? And it struck me, a bowling ball, now, that looks a hell of a lot like the old-fashioned kind of bomb, you know what I mean? So I thought I'd—"

"You're supposed to rub Menchik," Nick Rovito reminded him. "Not the whole goddam Bowlorama."

"Sure, so this is better. We can double up. Willy goes with Engel, see, and helps him dig it up, and then Engel rubs him and leaves him in the coffin with Charlie, and covers it all up again, and who's to find Willy? You gonna look for him in a grave?"

Nick Rovito smiled. He didn't do that very often, and it made all the boys around the table happy to see him do it now. "That's pretty nifty," he said. "I like the *feel* of that."

Somebody around the table said, "It's like a poetic humor, huh, Nick?" and Nick Rovito said, "Yeah."

Somebody else around the table said to Engel, "Maybe Charlie'd like that, huh, Engel? Somebody to pass the time with."

Somebody else around the table said, "You can throw in a deck of cards." He laughed when he said it, and everybody else around the table laughed except Engel and Nick Rovito. Nick Rovito smiled, which for him was the same as laughing. Engel looked glum. He looked glum because he felt glum.

Somebody around the table said, "They can play honeymoon bridge!" All the boys laughed again at that, and Nick Rovito even chuckled, but Engel still kept looking glum.

Nick Rovito said, "What's the matter, Engel? What's the problem?"

"Digging up a grave," said Engel. He shook his head. "I don't like the whole idea of it."

"So what are you, superstitious? It's a Catholic cemetery, there won't be no evil spirits around." All the boys laughed again, and Nick Rovito looked pleased with himself.

Engel said, "That isn't it. It's the work involved. It's manual labor, Nick."

Nick Rovito sobered up right away, knowing what Engel meant. "Look, kid," he said. "Look, if it was just a hole in the ground I wanted, I'd hire some bum to dig, am I right? But this is a special case, you know what I mean? I need somebody on the inside, and trustworthy, and young and strong enough so he don't get a heart attack himself when he starts in digging, you follow me? You're my right hand, Engel, you know that, you're my right arm. It's like I'm out there digging myself when you're out there digging."

Engel nodded. "I know that," he said. "I appreciate that. It was only the principle of the thing."

"I understand," Nick Rovito told him. "And don't you worry, you bring back that suit, there's a nice bonus in it for you."

"Thanks, Nick."

"Plus the geetus for rubbing Willy," said somebody else around the table. "Don't forget that, Engel."

Willy. That was something else, something Engel hadn't thought about yet. Except for Conelly, when it was kill or be killed and Engel was caught up in the suddenness and excitement of the whole thing anyway, Engel had never rubbed anybody in his life, which apparently all the boys around the table including Nick Rovito had now forgotten. Engel wasn't even sure he *could* rub somebody, just like that, in cold blood.

Still, he hadn't spoken up when the idea was first presented, and besides, Nick Rovito had looked so happy about it when it was suggested that Engel knew the worst thing he could do was try and wriggle out of it now, so, reluctantly, he said, "Yeah, about Willy. Where do I check out a gun?"

Nick Rovito shook his head. "No gun," he said. "You take your coat off to dig, he sees the gun, he's spooked. And a great big loud shot in a cemetery in the middle of the night, maybe somebody hears it, and you don't get time to fill the grave in again."

Somebody around the table said, "What the hell, Engel, you got a shovel."

"I got to hit him with the shovel?"

"Do it any way you want, kid. But no gun, that's all."

Engel shook his head. "What a job. I might as well be legit. Dig half the night and conk some guy on the head with a shovel. I might as well gone straight."

Nick Rovito said, "Don't talk like that, Engel. These little problems, they come along, that's all. Most of the time it's a good life, am I right?"

"Yeah, I guess so. You're right, Nick, I shouldn't complain."

"That's okay, kid. It's a shock, that's only natural."

Engel thought of something else then, and said, "I just thought of something else."

But Nick Rovito said, "In a second. About Willy. You know him?"

Engel nodded. "I seen him around. Trucker. Drives stuff to Canada for us sometimes."

"That's the one. So you tip him to the job yourself, okay?"

Engel nodded.

"Now, what was the other thing?"

"About the suit. You want the whole suit, or just the coat? I mean, where's the stuff sewed?"

Nick Rovito looked at Fred, and Fred said, "Just in the coat, that's all. In the lining of the coat."

"That's good," said Engel. "The way I feel about it, I wouldn't like the idea taking his pants off him."

Nick Rovito patted his shoulder. "Of course not! Whadaya think, kid? It was going to be something in bad taste, I wouldn't even ask, am I right?"

4

AS IF HE DIDN'T have troubles enough, Kenny gave him a car with standard shift. "What the hell, Kenny," he said, "what the hell do you call this?"

"A Chevy," said Kenny. "Just what you asked for. A Chevy, couple years old, black, mud smeared on the license plates, kind of dirty and inconspicuous to go with a Brooklyn locale, speed and acceleration not a factor, two shovels and a crowbar and a blanket in the trunk."

"But it keeps *stalling*" Engel told him. "I start it, and it jumps forward, and it stalls."

"Yeah?" Kenny came over and looked in the window and said, "Well, you don't have your foot on the clutch, that's what the problem is."

"My what? The what?"

"That dingus there, by your left foot."

"You mean this here is a *standard shift?*"

"It's the only car we got suits the requirements," Kenny told him. "You want a white convertible, a powder-blue limousine, a red Mercedes 190SL—"

"I want a quiet car!"

"You're sittin in it."

"You know how long it's been since I drove a standard shift?"

"You want a pearl-gray Rolls Royce, a pink and blue and turquoise Lincoln Continental, a gold and sea-green Alfa Romeo—"

"All right, never mind. Never mind, that's all."

"Anything you want, Engel, any car I got." Kenny made a large gesture to include the whole garage.

"I'll take this one. Never mind, I'll just take this one."

So all the way over to Brooklyn he kept stalling at red lights. It had been years since his left foot had done anything in a car but tap in time to the music from the radio.

It just fit in with the rest of the day, that's all. Like he was barely home to Carmine Street from the meeting when the phone rang, and not thinking it out first he made the mistake of answering. He'd had some sort of idea in his head it might be Nick Rovito calling to tell him the whole deal was off, but of course it wasn't, and as soon as he said hello, even before he heard a word from the telephone against his ear, he knew who it had to be.

And it was. "You were beautiful, Aloysius," his mother said. "I looked at you coming down them church steps with all those important men, and I said to myself, 'Would you believe it, Frances? Would you believe that was your son up there, so tall, so handsome, with such important men?' I was actually crying, Aloysius, the people around me actually thought I must be a relative I was crying so. And when I told them, 'No, I'm crying for happiness, that's my son out there with the coffin,' I got these very funny looks, how did I know how they'd take it?"

"Uh," said Engel.

"Did you see me? I waved a scarf, that one from the World's Fair? Did you see me?"

"Well, uh, I was kind of preoccupied up there. I didn't notice very much of anything."

"Oh. Well, that's all right." She sounded as though she meant she wasn't bleeding *too* badly. "Anyways," she said, brightening, "I got home in time to make you the most wonderful dinner you ever had in your life. Don't thank me, you deserve it, the least a mother can do . . ."

"Uh," said Engel.

"What? Don't say you're not coming, it's too late, everything's started. It's all in the oven already. Even a mince pie, special."

"I got a job to do," Engel said. He would have said so anyway, and it was only a pity it happened to be true. "There's something I'm supposed to do tonight for Nick Rovito."

"Oh," she said, this time sounding as though she meant she was bleeding *very* badly. "Your work is your work," she said doubtfully.

"Nothing I can do," he said.

And wasn't *that* the truth! Now, shortly after midnight, driving toward Brooklyn, he reflected on it and was bitter. What a job for an executive! Digging up graves in the middle of the night. Conking people on the head with shovels. Driving standard-shift cars. He drove grimly, forgetting most of the time to shift out of first, and got lost twice over in Brooklyn.

He'd contacted Willy Menchik after the conversation with his mother, and arranged to meet him outside Ralph's

Pub on Utica Avenue in Brooklyn at one A.M., but with the standard shift and getting lost and everything, it was twenty minutes past one before he got there.

He pulled to the curb in front of Ralph's, and a shadow disengaged itself from the wall and reeled over, tilting heavily to the left. It stuck Willy Menchik's narrow face through the open window on the passenger side, exhaled whiskey fumes all over the car, and announced, "You're late. You're twenny minutes late."

"I had a little trouble." Engel had remembered this time to put the gear lever in neutral. His left foot was pressed down on the clutch anyway, just to be on the safe side. "Get in," he said. "Let's get this over with."

"Righto." Willy straightened up, without getting his head out the window first. There was a crump, and a sigh, and Willy sank out of sight.

Engel said, "Willy!" There wasn't any answer. "He's drunk," said Engel, and nodded his head. That was all he'd needed.

He got out of the car, and walked around to the passenger side, and opened the door, and picked Willy up and dumped him onto the seat, and closed the door, and walked back around to the driver's side, and got behind the wheel, and tried to drive away in neutral. The motor roared, but they weren't going anywhere. He cursed, and tried to shift into first gear without puting his foot on the clutch. He made it, but then the car made a terrible noise, and leaped forward, and stalled. Willy rolled off the seat, hit his head on several things, and finished all crumpled on the floor under the dashboard.

Engel looked at him in exasperation. "Wait a while, will you?" he asked. "First you help me dig, okay? We'll conk your head to your heart's content later on, but first you help me dig, you got it?"

Willy was out, so didn't answer him. The car was out, too. Engel got it started again, and remembered about his left foot, and drove away from there.

He finally did get to the cemetery, around some cockamamie back way with the road under repair, and parked in pitch-blackness under a tree near the cemetery gate. He'd left Willy on the floor, figuring he couldn't fall anywhere from there, and now he turned on the inside light and started jabbing Willy in the kidneys to wake him up. "Willy! Hey! We're at the cemetery!"

Willy made a face, and groaned, and shifted around, and said, "Whadaya do?"

"We're at the cemetery. Come on."

"We're at the *what?*" Willy sat up, startled, and slammed his head into the dashboard, and went back down again.

"I might as well gone to college," said Engel, "like my mother wanted. I might just as well gone legit, and *took* the slings and arrows of outrageous fortune. So I got money, I got prestige, I got the respect of my community, I even got a pipe with my name on it at Kean's, but is it worth it? To be involved with slobs like this masochist on the floor here, is it worth it? To go dig up graves and conk people on the head with shovels and drive a standard-shift car and get lost forty times in Brooklyn and associate with slobs like Willy Menchik at this hour of the night, I might as well been a *milkman.*"

He opened the door and stepped out, still grambling. "I might better *off* been a milkman, they got a *union.*" But then he said, "Ahhhhhhggggggghhhhh," in disgust, because he knew it was worth it. Up till now, being Nick Rovito's right-hand man had been a simple and pleasant job. Make the phone calls, keep the appointment book, deal with the smaller matters of executive decision, it was like being the boss's son at an ad agency.

Yeah. And now after four years he was finding out that every once in a while, also like being the boss's son at an ad agency, there was going to be a grave to be dug up or somebody to be conked on the head with a shovel or a standard-shift car to be driven through Brooklyn, and then for a little while the job was going to be demeaning, actually demeaning. Even unsanitary.

Thinking about it, he walked around the car and opened the door and Willy fell out onto the ground and hit his head on a rock. Engel said, "Will you *stop* it? You keep on this way, you'll build up a *immunity,* and a shovel's all I got with me."

Willy groaned and rolled over, and when he rolled over, his head was just under the car. Engel saw what was coming, and grabbed Willy's ankles, and just as Willy's head was coming up Engel yanked him clear, and Willy sat up untouched for once, and made a face, and said, "Man, I got a headache."

"You're drunk, that's what your trouble is."

"So what are you? You sober?"

"Of course I'm sober. I'm always sober." Which was an exaggeration, but by comparison with Willy a very small one.

Willy said, "That's what I don't like about you, Engel, that goddam holier-than-thou attitude of yours."

"Come on, get on your feet, we're at the cemetery."

But Willy just sat there. He wasn't done talking yet. "You are the only guy I know," he said, "what would get the word to go out and dig up a grave in the middle of the night and *not* get drunk. You probably didn't even get drunk on V-J Day, that's the kind of guy *you* are."

"The kind of guy I am," Engel told him, "Nick Rovito tells me to go dig up a grave I don't sit on the ground and bitch about it."

"Brown-nose."

"What was that?"

Willy raised his head and squinted belligerently, moonlight on his face. Then all at once the belligerence faded away, and he looked baffled. He said, "What did I say?"

"That's what I want to know. You know who you're talking to?"

"Engel, I'm drunk. I'm not responsible. I apologize, Engel, I apologize from my bottom. From my heart. From the bottom of my heart."

"Come on, let's get started."

Willy sighed. Whiskey fumes drifted upward. "It's alius the same thing," he said. "I get to drinkin, I ran off at the mouth. One of these days I'm gonna talk myself into a lot of trouble, you mark my words. You just mark my words, that's all."

"Come on, Willy, on your feet."

"You'll watch out for me, won't you?"

"Sure."

Engel helped him to his feet. Willy leaned against the side of the car and said, "You're my buddy, that's what you are."

"Sure." Engel opened the car door and got the flashlight out of the glove compartment.

"Buddies," said Willy. "We *alius* been buddies, right from the beginning, huh, pal? Thick and thin, thummer and winter. Ever since good old PS One Eighty-four, ain't that right? Remember good old PS One Eighty-four?"

"I never went there."

"Whadaya talkin about? You and me was inseparable. In-*sep*arable!"

"Quit shouting. Here, hold the flashlight."

Engel handed him the flashlight, and Willy dropped it. "I'll get it, Engel, I'll get it!"

"You just stand there!" Engel got the flashlight and held it himself. He went around to the back of the car and opened the trunk. The tools were there, wrapped in an army blanket. "Come here, Willy, carry this stuff."

"Second. Second."

Engel flashed the light at him, and Willy was patting himself all over, like a man looking for a match. Engel said, "Whadaya got now? Bugs?"

"Pint," said Willy. "I had a pint." He fumbled the door open, and the inside light went on again. "Ahh!"

"Quiet!"

"Here it is! It musta fell on the floor somehow."

"Will you come here?"

"I'm on my way."

Willy slammed the door, and lurched to the rear of the car, and Engel flashed the light on the rolled army blanket. "Carry that stuff."

"Aye aye, sir." Willy saluted, badly, and gathered up the army blanket in his arms. "Ufff! Heavy!" The tools clanked together inside the blanket.

"Carry it on your shoulder. On your shoulder. Put it up on—let me—get it up on—up on your—*don't drop it!*"

Engel picked up the tools and the blanket, rolled them together again, and put the package on Willy's shoulder. "Now, *hold* it there!"

"Got it, Chief, got it. Rely on me, Chief. Got it right here."

"All right, let's go."

Engel shut the trunk, and they started away from the car, going through the cemetery gate and down a gravel pathway that made crunching sounds beneath their feet. Engel went first, shining the flashlight ahead of himself, and Willy came stumbling along behind him, the tools clanking together on his shoulder. After a minute Willy started to sing a song to the tune of "Maryland, My Maryland": "'One Eighty-four, One Eighty-four/You're the school that we adore;/One Eighty-four, One Eighty-four/In the *Bronx* on—'"

"Shut *up!*"

"Well, it's a very mournful place, that's all."

"Just shut up for a minute."

"Very mournful place." Willy began to snuffle.

Engel didn't know exactly where he was. He flashed the light around and led the way up one gravel path and down the other, and behind him Willy shuffled and snuffled and sometimes mumbled to himself. The tools made muffled clanking sounds inside the army blanket, their feet crunched on the gravel, and pale marble monuments crouched in the moonlight all around them.

After a while Engel said, "Ah. Up this way."

"Very mournful place," said Willy. "Not like California. You ever been to California?"

"It should be right over here."

"I never been to California. Some one of these days, you betcha life. 'Cal-i-forn-ia, *here* I come/Right back where—'"

"Shut *up!*"

"Yah, ya brown-nose."

"What?"

"You're makin all the noise yourself, ya bum. I saw through you way back in PS One Eighty-four. You were a brown-nose then, and you're a brown-nose now, and you'll be—"

Engel turned around and said, "Shut your little face, Willy."

Willy blinked five or six times and said, "What did I say?"

"You better start listening, that's what I say."

"You know what it is? It's the tension. This place gives me tension, and acidi-diddy. Acid indigestion."

"Put the tools down. We're here."

Willy looked around, open-mouthed. "Oh, yeah?"

"Put them *down.*"

"Oh, yeah." Willy stepped out from under the tools, and they hit the ground with a clang.

Engel nodded. "A real beaut," he said. "Next to you, that car is a magic carpet, next to you."

"What?"

"Never mind. Spread the blanket out."

"What the hell for?"

"To put the dirt on."

"Dirt?"

"That we dig up!"

"On the blanket? You'll get it dirty!"

"It's a *ground*cloth! So there won't be dirt on the grass to show somebody was digging here."

"Oohh! By golly, that's brilliant!"

"Will you spread the cloth? Will you just for Christ's sake spread the cloth?"

"The blanket, you mean."

"*Spread* it."

"Right, Chief."

Willy grabbed a corner of the blanket and yanked, to spread it. Tools went clattering this way and that. Willy said, "Woops."

"Never mind. That's all right. I don't even care."

"You're a good guy, Engel, you know that? You're a real pal."

"Yeah, yeah."

Engel flashed the light around. They hadn't put the sod down yet, so the brown rectangular outline of the grave showed clearly; that would make the job easier. Engel said, "I'll hold the flashlight, you dig. Then after a while we'll switch."

"Right, Chief."

"Throw the dirt on the blanket. You got it? On the blanket."

"On the blanket."

Engel watched mistrustfully, but Willy threw the first shovelful on the blanket, and the second, and the third. Engel backed up a few steps, sat on a tombstone, and held the light for Willy to dig by.

It took quite a while, longer than Engel had expected. After about twenty minutes he took over on the shovel and Willy held the light. Willy sat on the tombstone and opened his pint and began to cry. "Poor Whatsisname," he said. "Poor, poor Whatsisname."

Engel stopped digging and looked at him. "Who?"

"The guy down there. Under the ground. Whatsisname."

"Charlie Brody."

"Charlie Brody? You mean Charlie Brody? Old Charlie Brody's dead?"

"You knew it half an hour ago."

"Well, I'll be damned. Good old Charlie Brody. Did he owe me any money?"

"I wouldn't know."

"Naah. Nobody owes me any money. What do I get paid for this job?"

"Fifty."

"Fifty. Good old Charlie Brody. Fifty bucks. I'm gonna light a candle for Charlie, that's what I'm gonna do. Fifty bucks."

"Flash the light over here, will ya? What are you flashin it over there for?"

"I was drinkin."

"Is that right? Flash the light over here."

"OOOHHH, 'I dreamed I saw Joe Hill last night/As alive as you and—'"

"*Shut up!*"

"Ahhhh, ya brown-nose."

Engel ignored him this time, and just kept digging. Willy giggled for a while and then cried a while, and then whispered all the verses of "The Bastard King of England." When he was done, Engel gave him the shovel back, and took the flashlight, and Willy dug a while.

Willy was quieter when he was digging. He started to sing "Fifteen Men on a Dead Man's Chest," but he didn't have the wind for it while he was digging, so he quit. Engel lit a cigarette, and watched the pile of dirt beside the grave get higher and higher. He was going to have to put all that dirt back himself, without help. Wonderful.

Willy said, "Hey!"

"What?"

"I hit something! A treasure chest or something!"

"You don't suppose you hit the coffin, do you?"

"Oh, yeah. Look at that, I scratched it."

"That's a shame."

"That's a real nice wood, too. Look at that wood. Who'd bury nice wood like that? It's liable to rot."

Engel went over and looked down. Willy was standing in a hole shoulder-deep, with just a little of the coffin cleared of dirt. Engel said, "Finish getting the dirt off the top while I see can I find where you tossed the crowbar."

"You don't suppose I left it on the blanket, do you?"

"I wouldn't be a bit surprised."

Engel looked around, and found the crowbar over near the tombstone he'd been sitting on. He brought it back as Willy was finishing clearing dirt from the coffin. Engel said, "Here. There's two locks on it. Break them open, and then get me the suit coat."

Willy gulped and said, "You know what? All of a sudden, I'm scared."

"What are you scared of? You superstitious?"

"That's just what I am, I couldn't think of the word."

"Just break those two locks. Give me the shovel."

Willy handed the shovel up to him, then bent reluctantly to break the locks with the crowbar. Engel waited, hefting the shovel, looking at Willy's head. Willy broke the locks, and then stood there looking bewildered. "How do I open the top? I'm *standing* on the top."

"Get over on the edge."

"What edge? The top overlaps."

"Oh, hell. Get up here. Lie on the ground up here and reach down with the crowbar and lift the top up."

"Yeah, yeah."

It took a while to get Willy up out of the hole. He kept slipping back in, and threatening to drag Engel in with him, but finally Engel got a grip on the seat of his pants and dragged him out. Willy squirmed around, reached the crowbar down into the hole, and began fishing around with the crowbar for a grip on the lid. Engel stood on the other side of the grave, the shovel in one hand and the flashlight in the other.

Willy said, "Got it! Here it comes, here it—Flash your light down here, will ya, I can't see a thing."

Engel flashed the light down into the hole. The coffin lid was opened straight up, and inside was aft white plush. Engel stared.

The coffin was empty.

Willy shouted, "Oy! Oy!" He scrambled to his feet, shouting, "Oy! Oy!"

Engel knew he was going to run, he knew the little bum was going to ran. He dropped the flashlight, took a two-handed grip on the shovel, swung wildly, missed the departing Willy by two feet, lost his balance, fell into the hole, landed on the white plush, and the lid slammed down.

5

NICK ROVITO WAS NOT going to be pleased. Engel sat in the library of Nick Rovito's town house, surrounded by shelf after shelf of the books the interior decorator had picked out, and told himself Nick Rovito was not going to be pleased at all. In the first place he wouldn't be pleased because nobody is pleased to be gotten out of bed at four-thirty in the morning, but in the second place he wouldn't be pleased with what Engel had to tell him.

The last hour and a half had been somewhat hectic. After he'd struggled back out of that damn coffin, and wasted five minutes looking for Willy, he'd forced himself to take the time to fill in the hole again and smooth everything out and make sure there wasn't any sign left that anybody'd been there. Willy had gone off without his pint, which still contained an ounce or two, and Engel gulped it down gratefully, then tossed the pint in the hole and covered it up. When the grave was filled in again, he rolled the tools into the army blanket, found his way back to the car, and drove back to Manhattan, mostly in first.

Right now the car was in a no-parking zone out front, and Engel was sitting in the library waiting, while one of the bodyguards went to wake Nick Rovito. Engel smoked nervously, and wondered where Willy was by now. More important, he wondered where Charlie Brody was by now.

The door opened, and Nick Rovito came in, in a yellow silk dressing gown with his initials in chartreuse Gothic script on the pocket. Nick Rovito said, "So where's the coat?"

Engel shook his head. "I didn't get it, Nick. Everything went wrong. Willy's still alive, and I didn't get the coat."

"Is this Engel? Let me look at your face. Is this my right-hand man, my trusted assistant, the man to which I gave every opportunity and all my trust and confidence? This cannot be Engel, this must be a ringer in a funny face. Two things I ask from you and you don't do either *one?*"

"He wasn't there, Nick."

"Wasn't there, wasn't there, who wasn't there? Whadaya talking about, ya disappointment, ya, whadaya telling me?"

"Charlie, Nick. Charlie wasn't there."

"Charlie wasn't *where?*"

"In the coffin."

"What did ya do, ya ungrateful bastard, ya digged up the wrong coffin?"

Engel shook his head. "I digged—dug—digged up the right coffin, only Charlie wasn't in it. Nobody was in it."

Nick Rovito came closer and said, "Let me smell your breath."

"I had a shot afterward, Nick, but nothing beforehand, on a stack of Bibles."

"Are you sitting there and telling me we give that grand send-off to an empty *coffin?* Are you telling me three Congressmen and eight motion picture stars and the Housing Commissioner for the City of New York made a special trip in the middle of the week to pay their last respects to an empty *coffin?* Is that what you have the gall and the disrespect to come and tell me to my face?"

"I can't help it, Nick. It's the truth. Me and Willy dug it up and opened it, and there wasn't a damn thing in it. Willy got spooked and run off and I was too startled myself to grab him in time. In fact, I fell in."

"In fact, you did what?"

"I fell in. In the grave."

"Why'd you bother getting out? Will ya tell me?"

"I figured you ought to know what happened."

"So tell me what happened."

"Charlie wasn't there, and his suit wasn't there, and Willy got away."

"That ain't what happened, that's what *didn't* happen. So tell me what *happened*?"

"You mean, where's Charlie?"

"Yeah, that for openers."

Engel spread his hands helplessly. "I dunno, Nick. If we didn't bury him today, then I just don't know where he is."

"So find out."

"Like where?"

Nick Rovito shook his head sadly. "You are the biggest disappointment of my entire lifetime, Engel," he said. "As a trusted assistant, you are an abortion."

Engel frowned, trying to think. "I suppose," he said, "I suppose the thing to do *is* go talk to the undertaker."

"Mortician. He likes you should call him mortician."

"The mortician. I figure he's the last one to see Charlie's body, maybe he knows what happened to it."

Nick Rovito said, "If he didn't put it in the coffin, what the hell else would he do with it?"

"Maybe he sold it to a medical student."

"Charlie Brody? What the hell would a medical student want with Charlie Brody?"

"To experiment on, maybe. To make like a Frankenstein monster, maybe."

"A Frankenstein monster. *You're* a Frankenstein monster. I send you on a simple matter, get me a lousy suit coat, you come back with Frankenstein monsters."

"Nick, it isn't *my* fault. *I* was there. If Charlie'd been there, everything would of been okay."

Nick Rovito put his hands on his hips and said, "Let me tell you the story. Straight from the shoulder, cards on the table, no secrets between friends. You go out and you find me that coat. I don't give a damn where Charlie Brody's body is, and I don't give a damn about medical students or Frankenstein monsters, all I give a damn about is that coat. You *find* me that coat, Engel, or you go back out to Brooklyn where there's a nice empty coffin handy, and you dig it up again, and you climb in, and you shut the lid, and good-bye. Do I make myself clear?"

"What a business," said Engel.

"Business? You call this a business? I call it Olsen and Johnson, that's what I call it."

"Sometimes I think to myself, I could of gone in the army and retired at age thirty-eight."

Nick Rovito studied him thoughtfully for a second or two, and then his face softened. "Engel," he said, much more calmly than before, "don't talk that way. Don't mind what

48

I been saying, I'm just not used to this getting out of bed at four-thirty in the morning, and coffins with nobody inside, and grand send-offs with nobody sent off, and all the rest of it. I'm just not used to it, that's all."

"What the hell, Nick, it don't happen to *me* every day, either."

"I understand that. I put myself in your position, and I understand that, and I see you done everything you could of been expected to do, and you were right to come back here and tell me about it like this. After all, aren't you the man saved me from Conelly? Aren't you my right hand? I shouldn't of blown up at you like I done, because if it's anybody's fault it's Charlie Brody's, and it's just too bad the bastard's already dead, because if he wasn't you could kill him for me."

Engel said, "No, you were right to chew me out, I shouldn't of let Willy get away, that was poor organization on my part."

"The hell with Willy, that don't mean a thing. We'll get Willy by the end of the week anyway. If worst comes to worst, we'll let Harry get him at the Bowlorama. The important thing *is* the suit."

"I'll look for it, Nick, that's the most I can promise you, I'll look for it."

"You don't even need to say it, Engel, you know the way I feel about you. You are my trusted assistant, my altered ego, whither thou goest I am there in spirit. If anybody on God's green earth can find me that blue suit coat, you are the man."

"I'll do my best, Nick."

Nick Rovito laid a fatherly hand on Engel's shoulder. "Wherever that suit is," he said, "it ain't going anywhere before morning. You look tired, you been digging and everything, and—"

"Kenny gave me a car with standard shift."

"He did? What the hell for?"

"I'm not complaining, it was the only car he had suited the requirements."

"I didn't know they even made standard shift any more. Anyway, that's neither here nor there. The important thing is, you need your rest if you're gonna operate at peak perfection, so the thing for you to do is go home, get a good night's sleep, and when you're all rested you go out and see can you find the suit. Fair enough?"

"I could use some sleep, I guess."

"Sure you could. And don't mind what I said before, I was just upset, you know?"

"Sure, Nick." Engel got to his feet, and said, "Listen, I left the car out front. Could somebody else take it back for me? I'll grab a cab home from here, okay? I mean, my left foot's exhausted."

"Leave everything to me. Don't worry about the car or nothing, concentrate your energies exclusively on the suit. You'll do that for me?"

"Sure, Nick."

Nick Rovito patted his shoulder. "You're my boy."

6

THE SIGN ON THE front lawn that said

AUGUSTUS MERRIWEATHER
Grief Parlor

was three feet wide and in neon, but it was *blue* neon, for
dignity. Behind this sign and beyond the manicured lawn was
the building, a robber baron's town house when it was built
in the latter part of the nineteenth century, its gables and bay
windows all done in a rotten stucco now painted a gloomy
brown. A broad empty porch spread across the broad vacuous
face of the house, and as Engel came up the slate walk he saw
that this porch was full of uniformed policemen.

He broke stride for a second, but of course it was too late,
he'd already been seen. Trying his best to look nonchalant,
he came walking on.

There were maybe thirty of the cops on the porch, and
they didn't seem to have anything to do with Engel's presence
here. They were standing around in groups of three and four,
talking together in low voices. They were all wearing their
white Mickey Mouse gloves, and their uniform coats were
miserably tailored in the time-hallowed custom of the force,
and when Engel got over the jolt of seeing them all there, he

realized it had to be just another wake. Merriweather, no bigot, planted the departed on both sides of the law.

The glances that were turned on Engel as he went up the stoop and into the middle of the swarm of cops were curious but cursory. Nobody was very interested. Engel crossed the porch, opened the screen door, and bumped into a guy coming out. "Woops," said Engel.

The guy, flailing his arms around as he staggered off-balance, was a cop, short, stocky, middle-aged. His uniform sleeve was so covered with yellow stripes and chevrons and hashmarks it looked like the yellow brick road. He grabbed hold of Engel while he got his equilibrium back, and then he said, "That's o—Say! Don't I know you?"

Engel squinched his cheeks up as he took a cautious close look at the cop's face, but didn't recognize him as anyone who'd ever collared him or had dealings with him connected with the organization. "I don't think so," he said. "Not that I know of."

"I could swear . . ." The cop shook his head. "Well, it don't matter. You on your way in to see him?"

Engel might have said yes if he'd known who "him" was. Instead, he said, "No, I got business with the undertaker. Merriweather."

The cop hadn't yet let go of Engel's arm. Now he frowned, saying, "I could swear I've seen you some place. I never forget a face, never."

Engel worked his arm free. "Must be somebody else," he said, edging his way around the cop and through the doorway. "Must be somebody . . ."

"It'll come to me," the cop said. "I'll think of it."

Engel let the screen door close between them and grate-fully turned his back on the cop. He was inside at last, and the place looked exactly the same as for Charlie Brody's wake yesterday, except for the uniforms. But there was the same orange-brown semi-darkness, the same muffled Art Nou-veau appearance to everything, the same sickly scent of flow-ers, the same thick carpeting, the same sibilant whispering from the mourners.

Just inside the door, on the right, stood a podium and a man. The man was taller, the podium somewhat thinner, and both gave off the same sepulchral air of Gothic anemia. Both were mostly in black, with a white oblong at the top. The white oblong at the top of the man was his face, a chalky droopy affair like the face of a bleached basset hound. The white oblong at the top of the podium was an open book, in which the mourners were to inscribe their names. Next to the book, attached to the podium by a long purple ribbon, there lay a black pen.

Either the podium or the man said, in a bloodless voice, "Would you care to sign, sir?"

"I'm not with this crowd," Engel said, keeping his voice down. "I'm looking for Merriweather. On business."

"Ah. I believe Mr. Merriweather is in his office. Through those drapes there, and down the hall. Last door on the left."

"Thanks." Engel started that way, and a voice behind him said, "Say. Just a minute, there."

Engel turned his head, and it was the cop again, the one with the yellow brick road on his sleeve. He was pointing a finger at Engel, and he was frowning. "Were you ever a re-porter?" he asked. "Did you used to cover City Hall?"

"Not me. You got me mixed up with somebody else."

"I know your face," the cop said. "I'm Deputy Inspector Callaghan, that ring any bells?"

It did. Deputy Inspector Callaghan was the cop of whom Nick Rovito once said, "If that bastard would lay off of us and go after them Red Communists like a patriot ought, he'd end the Cold War in six months, the rotten bastard." Deputy Inspector Callaghan was the cop who years before, when Nick Rovito made the mistake of sending one of the boys around with a cash offer for Callaghan's loyalty, threw a hammerlock on the boy and double-timed him over to Nick Rovito's office and threw him over Nick Rovito's desk into Nick Rovito's lap and said, "This is yours. But I'm not." So the name did ring bells for Engel, alarm bells, plus sirens, horns, whistles and kazoos.

But Engel said, "Callaghan? Callaghan? I don't remember any Callaghans."

"It'll come to me," said Callaghan.

Engel smiled, a little weakly. "Be sure and let me know."

"Oh, I will. I will."

"That's good." Still smiling, Engel backed through the drapes and out of sight.

He was in a different world now, though just as dim and cluttered a one. Out ahead of him stretched the hallway, narrow and low-ceflinged. Two wall fixtures shaped sort of like candles contained amber light bulbs shaped sort of like candle flames, and these dim amber bulbs were the only source of light. The walls were painted a color that was maybe coral, maybe apricot, maybe amber, maybe beige; the woodwork was done in a stain so dark as to be almost black, and the floor was carpeted in dark and tortuous Persian. If a Pharaoh had died in A.D. 1935, the inside of his pyramid would have looked like this hall.

Along the right-hand wall were faded small prints of bare-breasted (small-breasted) nymphs cavorting amid Romanesque ruins in which white erect columns were prominent, and along the left-hand wall were doors, these in the same dark wood stain as the moldings. Engel walked down past all these to the one at the very end, shut like all the rest. He rapped a knuckle on it, got no response, and pushed the door open.

This was Merriweather's office all right, a small cramped crowded place with a window overlooking a garage wall. The most modern piece of furniture in the room was a roll-top desk. There was no one sitting at it, apparently no one anywhere in the room.

Engel shook his head in irritation. Now he'd have to go out and ask the podium where else Merriweather might be, and show himself to Callaghan again, and . . .

There was a shoe on the floor, down at the corner of the roll-top desk. A bit of black sock showed at the top of the shoe. There was a foot inside there.

Engel frowned at the shoe. He stepped forward a pace, all the way into the room, and leaned far to the left, until he could see around the angle of the desk, and there, sitting on the floor, wedged into a corner amid the furniture, slumped Merriweather himself, eyes and mouth wide open, all the life flown out of him. The golden hilt of the knife stuck into his chest glittered brilliantly against its background of the red-stained shirt front.

"Oh ho," said Engel. He assumed immediately and without reservation that this bumping off of the undertaker was connected somehow with the disappearance of Charlie Brody. Merriweather had been the last one to see Charlie Brody dead, so it figured he'd known something about Brody's disappearance, which was why Engel had come looking for him. That he was now himself bumped off confirmed Engel's theory as far as he'd taken it, and also indicated one or more others in on the scheme, whatever it was. Registering all this, Engel commented, "Oh ho."

And a female voice, harsh and cold, said, "What are you doing here?"

Engel spun around and saw, standing in the doorway, a tall thin frigid beauty dressed all in black. Her black hair was done in a thick single braid coiled around her head, in the Scandinavian manner. Her face was long and bony, the stretched skin white as parchment, devoid of make-up except for a blood-red slash of lipstick. Her eyes were dark, almost black, and her expression was haughty, cold, contemptuous. She had the palest, thinnest hands Engel had ever seen, with long narrow fingers ending in nails painted the same scarlet as her lips. She seemed about thirty.

She hadn't, obviously, yet seen the body tucked behind the desk, and Engel didn't know exactly how to break the news to her. "Well, I . . ." he said indefinitely, and motioned vaguely toward the former Merriweather.

Her eyes followed his movement, and widened. She stepped deeper into the room, the better to see, and Engel got from her a whiff of perfume that for some reason reminded him of green ice. Engel said, "He was . . . uh . . ."

Ten or fifteen years fell away from the woman's face, leaving her a child with wide eyes and slack jaw. "Criminy!" she said, in a voice much younger and squeakier than before. Then her eyes rolled up, her knees gave way, and she fell on the floor in a faint.

Engel looked from Merriweather sprawled dead on one side of him to the woman in black sprawled unconscious on the other, and decided it was time to leave. He stepped over the lady, went back to the dim hallway, and shut the door. After adjusting his tie and his jacket and his breathing, he walked nonchalantly back down the hall and through the drapes to the vestibule.

Man and podium were still in place, beside the front door. Solemn-faced coppers in dark uniforms speckled with lint moved in and out of the viewing room. Engel crossed toward the door, being silent and calm and unobtrusive, and the damn Callaghan popped up again, clutching at Engel's sleeve, saying, "Insurance company. You work for an insurance company."

Engel said, "No, no, you got me mixed up with . . ." And trying to get his arm back and keep moving toward the door.

"I *know* your face," Callaghan insisted. "Where do you work? What do you—?"

A shriek stopped everything. It made a sound like a freight train with its brakes on, and everybody froze, cops going in and out, Callaghan all a-clutch, Engel with his hand out toward the door.

With a creaking you could almost hear, every head turned toward where the sound had been. Now, in the utter silence afterward, everyone looked, and everyone saw the woman in black standing in the doorway, hands up and out dramatically to thrust away the drapes, lips and nails scarlet, face dead-white, gown black.

One pale slender hand moved, one ruby-tipped finger pointed at Engel. "That man," announced the shattered voice, "that man has killed my husband."

7

"ENGEL!" SHOUTED CALLAGHAN. HE released Engel's sleeve to snap his fingers, and then, belatedly, realized what the woman had just said. "Hey!" he shouted, and grabbed again.

But it was too late. Engel was already through the doorway and halfway across the lawn. He vaulted the *Grief Parlor* sign, attained the sidewalk, and ran for dear life.

Behind him, voices shouted, "Stop him!" Behind him, cheap lumpy black shoes from the Army & Navy Store thudded in his wake. About half a block behind him and coming strong was a pack of patrolmen of all shapes and all sizes, all alike in their blue uniforms and white gloves and red faces.

Engel crossed a major street, against the light, being narrowly missed by a city bus, a TR-2, a *Herald Tribune* truck and a Barracuda. Behind him, the intersection was abruptly a sea of chaos, with cops and cars snarling together like long hair when it's been washed. Half the cops halted in the middle of the street and held their hands up to stop traffic so the other half could go through, but the second half couldn't get through because the first half was blocking the way. So were the city bus and the Barracuda, both of which had stalled. So was a Mustang, which had ran into the tail of the Barracuda.

So was a bohemian-looking young lady on a motor scooter, who had stopped in the middle of everything to see what was going on.

Still, most of the cops managed to get across the intersection and take up the chase again, hallooing to Engel to stop, to give himself up, to cease from resisting arrest.

Engel, meanwhile, had ran nearly a full block farther, and was beginning to get a stitch in his side. Ahead of him, at the corner, a young student policeman in gray-blue uniform and blue hat was talking into a police phone on a telephone pole. As the noise of the chase reached his ears he leaned slightly to one side, so he could see around the pole, and, with the telephone still to his ear, goggled at Engel running full tilt toward him and a capering mass of men in blue coming on strong behind.

Engel saw the student cop, saw him react, saw him speak hurriedly into the telephone and hang it up, saw him grip his nightstick and come warily out from behind the telephone pole, and saw a yawning alley to his left, between two ware-houses or factory buildings. Engel turned on a dime and pelted down the blacktop into the alley.

The sides were grimy brick, extending up half a dozen stories. The end was wood, weathered vertical slats ten or twelve feet high, a rickety-looking wall bowed outward in the middle up above.

In the middle down below there was a door, at the moment shut. Engel raced toward it, reminding God that he *hadn't* killed Merriweather and that he *had* been in church just yesterday morning, and when he got to the door it opened to his push. He stepped through and shut the door behind him.

Well, well. On this side there was another alley, with a large black truck idling in the middle of it, its engine chugging quietly to itself. There was also a long thick wooden bar leaning against the rear alley wall, and on both sides of the door through which Engel had just come, there were brackets apparently designed for the bar. Engel tried the bar and it worked beautifully, sealing the door shut.

Scant seconds after he'd sealed the door the shouting, charging mass of constables surged against it with a series of thuds. The door held. The wall, though wobbly-looking, was supported on this side by cross beams and end braces, and it too held.

A hammering commenced, and shouts of "Open up!"

Extending along the rear wall from the door rightward to the side wall was a stack of oil drums lying on their sides, the stack higher than Engel's head. A few odd sticks and some rope kept the stack from collapsing. Engel yanked a stick, tugged at two ropes, and the oil drums, with a rumble, came rolling down across the doorway, completely blanketing the rear of the alley. It would take a team of men twenty minutes to clear enough of those away to get at the door.

"Open up! Open up! Open in the name of the law!"

Engel moved on.

This alley was somewhat wider than the other, but still he had to snake along sideways next to the truck, which was facing out, its closed back toward the wall where all the thumping and yelling was coming from, and when he got to the truck cab and found it empty he promptly climbed aboard, remembered about putting it into first gear, and drove it out of the alley.

It took less than a minute to drive it around the block and back it into the alley on the other side, which was still alive at its deeper end with cops, including the pupil patrolman, who was lustily hammering away at the barred and blockaded door with his nightstick. None of the cops noticed when a big black truck which fitted the alley opening the way a cork fits a wine bottle was gently nudged and wedged into place, rear end first. Not, that is, until it was too late.

As Engel shut off the truck engine and pocketed the key, a new chorus of shouts erupted from the alley, more outraged, more desperate and more furious than before.

Engel walked calmly away, dropping the truck ignition key down the sewer at the corner, which appeared to be in a state of turmoil. Next to a Barracuda and a Mustang, which were locked nose to tail, two young men in sport coats were fighting. A lot of people were standing around a city bus, which apparently refused to start. Two police cars, with red dome lights circling, helped to block the intersection, while the four patrolmen who had been in them stood around a bohemian-looking young lady on a motor scooter, who was explaining to them at great and inaccurate length exactly what had happened. A growing mass of people and vehicles was forming a great circle about these foci, and the rumors at the outer fringes of this circle were fantastic. One group, in fact, under the impression that the crowd had formed to watch someone on a ledge, was wagering back and forth as to whether that someone would or would not jump.

"Excuse me," said Engel. "Pardon me. Excuse me." He worked his way through the crowd on one side, around the tussling young men, past the bohemian-looking young lady and the four fascinated fuzz, around the stalled bus with its irritated riders and apoplectic driver, through the crowd on the other side, and on the rest of the way back to the grief parlor.

He still had questions to ask.

8

THE PORCH STOOD EMPTY. In the viewing room the departed reclined unviewed. But just inside the main door the podium and the man, trustworthy sentinels, still stood at their posts. Engel said to them, indiscriminately, "The police sent me to talk to Mrs. Merriweather, find out what this is all about. Where is she?"

"I'm not sure, sir. I haven't seen her go out, so I imagine she's in the back part of the house *some*where, or possibly upstairs."

"Right."

Engel moved off, through the drapes and down the hall, opening doors. There wasn't much time. His plan, simply, was to find Mrs. Merriweather, kidnap her, take her somewhere safe and quiet, find out what she knew, if anything, about Charlie Brody and about who else would have had access to Charlie's body, convince her that he hadn't after all bumped off her husband, and return her to the grief parlor. But first, of course, he had to find her.

He opened every door he came to along the hallway, and they led, in order, to a cloakroom, a broom closet, a small windowless room full of stacked folding chairs, an equally small and windowless room stacked with coffins, a black staircase leading down, a yellow staircase leading up, and the office. All of these were empty, except for the office, and Merriweather was the only one there.

So. Upstairs, then, resting and recuperating from her shocking discovery. Engel went up the yellow stairs.

Here was yet another of the grief parlor's many worlds. This one was yellow and pink, chintz and terrycloth, light and airy as a toilet-paper commercial, with frills and laces everywhere. Early American bedspreads on beds with Colonial headboards. Bright wallpaper with designs of flowers and leaping figures. A pink hairy toilet-seat cover and pink hairy bathroom rug to match. Throw rugs on waxed floors. The gleam of polished maple everywhere. But no Mrs. Merriweather.

Farther up? Engel found the stairs to the attic and went up to find it a dark barren dusty wooden tent-shape, alive with wasps. Engel sneezed and went back downstairs.

She had to be somewhere. Her husband had just been killed, she'd just reported it to the cops, she had to stick around. Engel prowled the second-floor bedrooms again, still finding no one, went back down to the first floor, and finally decided, because there was no place else to look, to try the cellar.

There was a light switch on the wall at the head of the black stairs leading down. Engel turned it on, and light down there revealed that the stairs were wood and the floor below was concrete painted deck-gray. He went down to a mad scientist's laboratory. Coffins, steel tables, racks of bottled fluids, tubes and pipes and hoses. A large door led to a walk-in freezer, like those in butcher shops, this one containing several slabs, on two of which figures reclined under sheets. Engel lifted the sheets, but they were both strangers.

He went upstairs again and out to the front door, where podium and man stood like declarations of permanence and immortality amid the mortal clay. Engel said, "You sure she didn't go out?"

"Who was that, sir?"

"Mrs. Merriweather. Tall woman in black."

"I beg your pardon, sir?"

Engel, exasperated, went over and looked in the viewing room, but only the former Whatsisname was on view. He went back to podium and man. "I'm looking for Mrs. Merriweather," he said.

"Yes, sir, I know. If she isn't here, perhaps she isn't back from shopping. She went shopping this morning, and . . ."

"She was here ten minutes ago! A tall woman in black, right over there by the drapes."

"A tall woman in black, sir?"

"Mrs. Merriweather. Your boss's wife."

"No, sir. I'm sorry, sir, but no. Mrs. Merriweather is not a tall woman in black. Mrs. Merriweather is an exceedingly short and stout woman, and is usually in pink."

Engel said, "What?"

"Pink," said the podium. Or the man.

9

THERE WAS A NOTE on his apartment door, down on Carmine Street. It was written with Chinese-red lipstick on a large sheet of paper and stuck to the door with a false fingernail. It read: Honey, I'm back from the Coast. Where are you, baby, don't you want to see your Dolly any more? Leave a message with Roxanne's service.

Your sugar tongue,
DOLLY

Engel blinked at the message, at the reference in its finale to an old private joke he'd once upon a time shared with Dolly, and at the golden implications beckoning to him from the lipsticked paper. He plucked the false fingernail, turned the paper over, and saw that Dolly had used one of her résumés, a listing of the clubs and theaters where she'd worked. Dolly was what she called an exotic dancer, which is a dancer who gradually dances out of her clothing, and she was one of the fringe benefits Engel had derived when he'd made the big leap, four years ago, to Nick Rovito's right hand.

Holding Dolly's résumé in one hand and the false fingernail in the other, Engel nodded to himself with cynical detachment. This, he told himself, was the way things always went.

At any other time, any other time, he'd have left a message for Dolly in a minute, have gotten together with her by sundown today, and . . . and so much for the timing of destiny's bounty. Resignedly, bitterly, he crumpled note and nail into one hand, and with the other unlocked his way into his apartment.

The phone was ringing, speaking of timing. He dropped note and nail on the small table beside the door, glanced at himself in the oval mirror above the table to see if his expression was as disillusioned as he thought it was (it was), walked across the pale beige broadloom carpet on which bearskins and small rectangular Persians and occasional outsize orange cushions were scattered, picked up the phone from the end table beside the white leather sofa, and said, "I can't talk to you now, Mom, I'm working."

"I'm only your mother," she said. "So two nights in a row I cook you the kind of meal you never get, not because I'm like one of those mothers you see on television that's always interfering, eat a little chicken soup, *that* sort of mother, you know I'm not. But because of a special occasion, and I was proud of you yesterday beyond my wildest dreams, and I wanted to express my admiration and appreciation in the only way I can, which is cookery, the only thing I've ever done well. And now on *both* nights you aren't coming?"

"What? What both nights?"

"Last night," she said, "and tonight."

"Mom, I am working. This *is* no lie, this is no excuse, I am working. I am working harder and with more problems than ever before, and I can't talk to you now. I got to make some phone calls."

"Aloysius, I'm not merely your mother, you know that, I am also your confidante, your sharer of the ins and outs of the world, just like I was with your father even though he never did attain such heights as you, but the son always does exceed the father, that goes without saying."

"I can't talk about this on the phone," Engel told her.

"So come to dinner. You've got to eat dinner some place, why not here?"

"I'll call you when this is over. Right now I got to make some important phone calls, if I don't I'm in trouble."

"Aloysius—"

"I'll call you when I get a minute free."

"If you—"

"I promise."

"You wo—"

"I won't forget."

When this time she didn't have anything immediately to say, but let two or three seconds of silence elapse, Engel said, "Bye now, Mom, I'll call you," and promptly hung up. Just as promptly he picked up the receiver again, preparing to dial, and heard a tinny voice saying, "Aloysius? Aloysius?"

She hadn't hung up, and until she did the connection wasn't broken. Quickly Engel put the receiver down again. He counted to ten, then cautiously picked the receiver up, and this time he heard the precious dial tone.

He called Nick Rovito's office, but was told that Nick Rovito personally wasn't there. Engel identified himself and said, "Tell him it's urgent, and I'm at home, and would he call me right away."

"Right."

Next he called a man named Horace Stamford, once upon a time an attorney of some reputation, but, since his disbarment, upgraded to being the man in charge of the legal end of the organization's affairs. When he got Stamford on the line, Engel said, "I'm going to need a cover for this afternoon."

"Details," said Stamford. He prided himself on his speed, accuracy, detachment and planning ability, and therefore spoke in clipped sentences, like a telegram from someone who didn't know much English.

Engel gave him the details of his day's activities, not bothering to explain why he'd been doing what he'd been doing. It wasn't a part of Stamford's job to know that. He merely told him about going to the funeral parlor, about finding Merriweather dead and being identified by Callaghan and being pointed at by the woman who claimed to be Merriweather's wife but wasn't and making his escape. Then, "Callaghan took a long time to get a fix on me," he said, "and I don't think he's really sure yet. Besides, when they find out the woman who pointed at me wasn't the dead guy's wife after all, that'll confuse them more. So all I need is a cover for this afternoon."

Arranging cover *was* a part of Stamford's job. Engel listened as Stamford clucked to himself at the other end of the line, shuffling papers and so on. Finally Stamford said, "Races. Trotters. Freehold Raceway over in Jersey. You went with Ed Lynch, Big Tiny Moroni and Felix Smith. You picked one winner, Toothache, in the third race, at four to one. You had ten dollars on her. You had lunch in the American Hotel in Freehold; steak. You went down in Moroni's new car, a Pontiac Bonneville convertible, white. The top was down. You took the Lincoln Tunnel, the Jersey Turnpike and Route 9, and retraced exactly. You'll be arriving back in the city in five or ten minutes. They'll let you off at 34th Street and Ninth Avenue and you'll take a cab downtown. Got it?"

"Got it."

"Good." Stamford hung up.

So did Engel, and the phone immediately rang. He picked it up and said, "Nick?"

But it was his mother's voice that said, "We got cut off, Aloysius. And now I been getting a busy signal."

"We didn't get cut off," he told her. "I hung up. And I'm going to do it again. And you do it, too. I'll talk to you when I get a chance, right now I'm waiting for a call from Nick Rovito and I can't tie up the phone."

"Aloysius—"

"Hang up or I move to California."

"Oh!"

This was an old threat, but a seldom-used one, reserved for final emergencies when all else had failed. When all the appeals of fact, of logic and of emotion had been exhausted, there was at last the specter of California. Once Engel mentioned California, his mother knew at once and without question that he was serious and that what he wanted was important.

But the funny thing was, the threat to move to California was hollow where everything else Engel had said, about working and about waiting for the call from Nick Rovito, was real. Engel hated California, would rather have lived in Sing Sing than California, and desired nothing of California other than that it stay peaceably where it was, on that other coast, three thousand miles away.

And yet he knew, if the day should ever come when this ultimate threat, too, was ignored by his mother, he would no longer have any choice. He would have to move to California. The alternative—staying in New York with *no* ultimate defense against his mother—was the only thing he could think of worse than living in California.

At the moment, though, the threat was still potent. "Oh!" said his mother, when he voiced it. "If it's important, I won't interrupt. Call me when you get a minute."

"I will," Engel promised, and this time they hung up together.

While waiting for the call from Nick Rovito, Engel went on into the bedroom and changed his clothes, since the rushing around he'd had to do had left him feeling a bit rumpled. He wished he could take a shower, but there wasn't time. Besides, Nick Rovito might call while he was in there, and he wouldn't hear the phone ring.

Engel's apartment had originally been owned by a darling boy of a thing who designed costumes for Broadway musicals, and who had sold most of his furniture to the second owner, a television producer of strongly heterosexual if not marital bent, who replaced some of his predecessor's more flighty peaks of imagination with equipment more suited to his own personality: the bar and white leather sofa in the living room, the mirror on the bedroom ceiling, the movie projector set into one of the living-room walls, the master light switch on the end table beside the sofa. When Engel in his turn had moved in, buying the furnishings from the TV man—who was, come to think of it, moving to California, as had the designer before him—he made yet a few changes of his own. He added a false back to a bedroom closet, sound-proofed the small room off the bedroom which neither of the former tenants had found any use for but in which Engel could now hold business discussions with absolute security—the way the law tapped phones and bugged private homes these days was not only illegal it was absolutely immoral—added the paintings of famous horses to the bedroom walls, put an electric garbage disposal in the kitchen and had strong wire mesh put on the outside of all the windows. By now the apartment was complex, fascinating and bewildering. The main colors throughout were purple and white and black and green. The designer's candelabra sat on the producer's bar next to Engel's electric drink dispenser.

From this last, Engel, in fresh clothing, dispensed himself a drink, then prowled the apartment and waited for the phone to ring. He was wearing slacks now, and a sport shirt, and casual Italian shoes with crepe soles. The ice tinkled in the glass he held, and anyone seeing him would have said, "Rising young executive in some sort of interesting business." Which would have been perfectly accurate.

Engel was on his second drink before the phone rang. He strode across the living room, stood beside the sofa, and picked up the receiver.

It was Nick Rovito. "I got your message, kid. How's tricks?"

"Bad, Nick."

"No suit?"

"No suit, and complications. The undertaker needs an undertaker."

"Mortician. He likes you should call him mortician."

"Mortician, undertaker, he could use either one."

"Am I following you, Engel?"

"Yes. Also, there's a woman involved, I don't know who she is. Tall, slender, good-looking in an icy way, played me and a whole bunch of cops for suckers and then cut out."

"Don't give me no details," Nick Rovito said. "All I want is results, or instead, a general picture about how results are on the way."

"It's getting complicated, Nick."

"Then make it simple. The simple thing is, Nick Rovito wants the suit."

"I know, Nick."

"It ain't the profit, it's the principle. Nick Rovito don't get robbed."

Engel knew that when Nick Rovito started talking about himself in the third person it meant his pride was hurt, his back was up, and his mind was set. So all he said was, "I'll get it, Nick, I'll get the suit."

"Good," said Nick Rovito. *Click,* said the phone.

Engel hung up. "The suit," he muttered to himself. He looked around the room, as though to find it somewhere here, maybe hanging on the back of a chair or draped over a bar stool. "Where the hell," he said aloud, "am I going to find that goddam suit?" When he got no answer, he drained his glass and turned toward the bar to make himself another drink.

Halfway there he was detoured by the sound of the door-bell ringing: a chimed quote from "L'Après-midi d'un faune," an inheritance from the designer. Frowning, Engel set the empty glass down on the bar, went out to the foyer, and opened the door.

Standing there was the mystery woman, all in black. "Mr. Engel?" she said, and smiled prettily. "May I come in? I believe I owe you an explanation."

10

WAS SHE TWENTY? WAS she thirty-five? More or less or in between? There was no way to tell.

Again, was she insane, or was she merely mindless, or some combination of the two? And again, as yet there was no way to tell.

Engel closed the door after she'd stepped into the apartment, and followed her into the living room, which she admired by turning around in a smiling circle and saying, "What an interesting place! How fascinating! How original!"

If there was one thing life had taught Engel, it was Wait and See. Don't ask, don't assume, don't jump the gun, don't try to hurry the world along, just Wait and See. If Madame X here intended to give him an explanation, fine; she'd do it at her own speed and in her own way, and in the meantime Engel would have an unusually fine opportunity to practice Wait and etc. So, coming into the living room after her, he merely said, "You want a drink?"

"Scotch sour?"

"Scotch sour. Right."

A Scotch sour was unfortunately not one of the drinks he could dial on his electric dispenser, so, as he went around behind the bar, he snaked out the drink guide he'd brought home one time from the liquor store, leafed through it hurriedly while keeping it hidden under the bar, and said, "Sit down, why don't you? I'll just be a minute."

It was a good thing he'd maintained his predecessor's tradition of a broadly stocked bar, including the refrigerated compartment underneath. A Scotch sour, it seemed, required one each of almost everything he had. While he assembled it, feeling like the witch in "Snow White," his guest wandered around the living room, admiring the furnishings and the objects on the walls; a murky lightning-streaked abstract entitled "Summer Storm Fire Island" (designer), a primary-hued naturalistic portrait of a sad-faced clown (producer), and matched plaques of ducks in flight (Engel's mother). "How catholic! How unusual!"

Engel made himself a fresh Scotch and water and carried the two drinks over to where she stood by a side table, admiring its burden of fat red candles (designer) and fat orange oriental wood carvings (producer), plus this week's issue of *Time* (Engel). "Scotch sour," said Engel.

"Ah!" She spun around like a high school girl, all smiles and dimples, but the hand with which she took the drink was pale white and so slender as to be almost bony. But not unpleasantly so, no, not at all unpleasantly so. "Thank you," she said, and raised the glass, and over it batted at him eyes that belonged to no high-schooler. And the voice? Husky one instant, lilting the next, always interesting.

"Well sit," suggested Engel, and motioned at the sofa.

"Fine," she said, and moved at once to a Victorian chair with wooden arms and a seat covered in purple burlap. There she sat, crossed long legs with a nylon rustle, tugged at the hem of her black skirt to cover her knee, and said, "Now we can talk."

"Good." Engel settled himself on the sofa.

"What I can't understand," she said, smiling brightly at him, "is how one man can be so eclectic."

Engel couldn't understand it either, since he didn't know the word, so he said, "How did you find me?"

"Oh," she said, offhand, airily waving the hand with the glass in it, "I heard that policeman say your name, and I asked around, and here I am."

"Asked around where?"

"Police Headquarters, of course." She sipped at her drink, giving him the eyes again over the rim of the glass. "I've just come from there."

Engel automatically glanced toward the front door. If his sense of timing was right there'd be cops at that door within about half an hour now. Callaghan and company would be slowed down by their imprisonment in the alley, and further slowed down by the confusion of identities back at the grief parlor, but sooner or later they'd get themselves organized and on the move, and when that happened a couple of their foot soldiers would stop by here just to check. Not that they'd expect to find him here, but just because they liked to think of themselves as thorough. The phantom lady's mention of Police Headquarters reminded him of this, and so he automatically glanced toward . . .

Come from there?

He said it aloud: "*Come* from there? Police Headquarters?"

"Well, of course." She lowered the glass from her lips, and smiled at him with the wattage and intensity of a toothpaste ad. "I couldn't leave everything all mixed up, could I?"

"Oh, no," he said, "of course not. You couldn't do that."

All at once the smile shrank from her face, and her expression became troubled. "Isn't there," she said, a new vibrato trembling in her voice, "isn't there enough sadness and worry and confusion in the world already?"

"I'd say so," he said.

"So as soon as I recovered," she said, the tremolo lessening but still slightly present, "and realized what I'd done, I went straight to Police Headquarters. They didn't know a thing about it yet, and they had a terrible time finding all those policemen who were chasing you, but I did explain things and they won't chase you any more after this. They promised me."

"They promised you."

"Yes." The smile flashed on again, like a searchlight being switched on, and she said, "The police are really very sweet, when you get to know them."

"I wouldn't know."

"Of course," she said, "*they* couldn't understand why you'd run away like that if you hadn't done anything wrong, but I understood it right away."

"You did."

"Well, of course. All at once someone accuses you of something perfectly dreadful, and a whole *army* of policemen start running at you . . . I'd have run away myself."

"But you explained it," said Engel. "You went to the cops and explained it so they won't chase me."

"Well, I thought I should. I thought it was my duty." She sipped, eyed, smiled, said, "You make a really fine Scotch sour, really fine."

"I wish," Engel told her, "I kind of wish you'd explain it to me. What you explained to the cops."

"Well, that's why I'm here. You see, when my—Oh. May I have another of these first?"

"Sure. Sure." Engel got to his feet, took the empty glass from her outstretched hand, and went back over behind the bar. He'd left the drink guide open, and now he began again to assemble the drink. One cocktail shaker, half full of cracked ice . . .

The mystery woman came over, undulating slowly across the room like something seen through water, and hitched herself gracefully onto one of the purple-topped bar stools. "You're really a very interesting man," she said.

. . . one part bar syrup . . .

"And I can't tell you how sorry I am if I caused you any inconvenience."

"No, that's all right. As long as it all comes out right in the end." . . . two parts lemon juice . . .

"I just can't believe you're a gangster. Oh! Was that a terrible thing to say?"

Engel looked up from his preparations. "Is that what they told you at Police Headquarters?"

She had both elbows propped on the bar, forearms vertical and fingers entwined, delicate chin resting on her grouped hands, lips smiling again and eyes being . . . provocative. "They told me you were a desperate character," she said. "They told me you were in the Mafia and Cosa Nostra and the Syndicate and I don't know what all."

"Diners' Club? Did they mention Diners' Club? Or the Masons?"

She laughed, a tinkly sound. "No, they didn't. I can see they gave me a slanted report on you."

"They're prejudiced." . . . eight parts Scotch; two, four, six, eight . . .

"I don't think you're a gangster at all."

"No?" . . . shake vigorously . . .

"I think you're charming."

"Yes?" . . . shake . . .

"Yes, I do. Like Akim Tamiroff on the Late Late Show. Only taller, of course, and without the mustache. And no accent. And your face is thinner. But the *feeling* is the same."

"Is it?" . . . vigorously.

"I've never told you my name, have I?"

Strain into whiskey-sour glass. "No, you haven't."

"Margo," she said. "Margo Kane."

"Engel," he said, in his turn. "Al—uh, Al Engel."

"Yes, I know. How do you do?" She extended a hand, high, the way women do.

For such a thin hand, it was very warm. Like holding an undernourished but attractive bird. "How do you do?"

"Fine, thank you."

Engel released her hand and went back to the drink. Garnish with cherry . . .

"Fine, that is," she went on, "all things considered. My bereavement and all."

. . . and a slice of lemon.

Engel set the completed drink up on the bar in front of her. "Bereavement? What bereavement?"

"Well, that's actually part of what I was going to tell you. It's all part of the same thing." Long pale fingers closed around the glass, lifted it to scarlet lips. "Mmmm. You *do* have the touch."

Engel was making a fresh drink for himself now, a much simpler process: an ice cube, a splash of Scotch, a dash of water. "You've had a bereavement?" he said, trying to get her back onto the subject.

"Yes." A wistful, sad, forlorn look came into her eyes. She tapped the long nails of her left hand on the bar just once, in a ripple, as though expressing the finish of something. "My husband," she said. "He died quite suddenly yesterday."

"Oh. I'm sorry to hear that."

"Yes. It was quite a shock. So sudden, so terrible, and so unnecessary."

"Unnecessary?"

"Yes. He was hardly an old man. Fifty-two. He should have had years and years of life ahead of—I'm sorry, I'll be all right in a minute."

A small white lace handkerchief had appeared in her hand, and tears in the corners of her eyes. She touched them away, shook her head slightly as though upset with herself for having thus given in to emotion, and took a strong swallow of her Scotch sour. "It's such a terrible thing," she said.

Engel was calculating. The husband had been fifty-two, and he by now doubted the wife could be more than twenty-seven or twenty-eight. It was the black clothing contrasting with the white skin that made her seem older at times. He said, "What was it, a heart attack?"

"No. An accident. One of those stupid . . . Well, there's no point going over and over it, it's happened and there's an end to it."

"You said," Engel reminded her, "that I'd killed him. That's how you sicked the cops on me."

"I don't know what came over me when I did that," she said, and looked lost and bewildered. She touched the back of her hand to her brow.

Engel felt like saying he did know what had come over *him* when she said that, because what had come over him had been cops, but she was too easily distracted from her main line of thought, so he said nothing. He just waited, looking attentive.

"I had come to see Mr. Merriweather," she said, as though recounting something sad that had happened long, long ago in the dim past, "to talk about the details of the funeral. Of course, my mind was full of thoughts about my husband, and how stupidly unnecessary his death had been—a kind of murder, in a way, murder by Fate, by Destiny, what you will—we never know what life has in store for us around the next cor—"

"Merriweather," Engel suggested. "You'd come to see him about the funeral."

"Yes. And then, seeing him there, lying there actually murdered, not by Fate but by some *person,* I suppose I just snapped for a minute."

"You snapped," said Engel. The way she kept skipping from style to style, from age to age, from mood to mood, he could believe she'd snapped for a lot longer than a minute.

"That must have been it," she was saying. "You were there, and I got you all confused with Destiny, and poor Mr. Merriweather mixed up with my husband, and just everything all confused."

"I'll say."

"I passed out—well, you know that—but when I came to I believe, I truly believe, I was no longer in my right mind. It seemed to me somehow it was my Murray who'd been murdered—" She passed a hand again across her brow, and said, "I can still remember just what I was thinking, and how sensible and natural and right it seemed at the time. Murray had been murdered, and in my mind's eye I saw the face of his murderer, and it was you."

"Just because I happened to be there," said Engel.

"Yes. It was just another—accident." A shadow crossed her face at the words, but then she shook her head and went on: "As soon as I regained consciousness, I tottered away to seek help, and when I saw you standing there by the door I . . . I said what I did." Contrition shone in her face now, and embarrassment. "I'm sorry."

Engel said, "You explained this to the police."

"Oh, yes. They were angry at first, but finally they said they did understand how it could have happened."

"You talked to Deputy Inspector Callaghan?"

"Not in person, no. On the telephone. He was still on his way to Headquarters when I left."

"Excuse me one second," Engel said. "I got to make a phone call."

"Certainly."

Engel came out from behind the bar, crossed the room to the phone, and dialed Horace Stamford again. As he stood there waiting for the call to be completed, he observed casually how tastefully the Widow Kane perched on a bar stool, one slender shapely leg crossed over the other, black-sheathed rump rounding neatly onto the purple plush.

Then Stamford came on. Engel identified himself and said, "The machine we talked about before. Has it started operating yet?"

"No, not yet."

"Then cancel."

Stamford asked no questions. Accuracy was his forte, not knowledge. "Will do," he said.

Engel hung up and went back over to the bar, this time sitting on the stool next to his guest. "Business," he said.

"Gangster business, I suppose." She looked at him appraisingly, a friendly smile on her lips. "It's so hard for me to think of you—"

She was interrupted by the sound of the fawn's afternoon. Her eyes widened, and she said, "I can't be found here!"

"What? Why—?"

"Murray's sisters! They'll try to break the will anyway, I know they will, bringing up a lot of ancient history, trying to smear me, tell lies about me, insinuations, *you* know the kind of thing." The fawn announced his afternoon again, making her rush: "If I'm found here, the day after Murray died, in the apartment of a strange bachelor—!"

"In back," Engel told her. "Go hide in the bedroom. Or the office back there, the little room with the soundproofing, that'd be best."

"Oh, bless you! You're so kind, so . . ." There was probably more, but she was already leaving the room.

Once Engel could no longer see or hear her, he headed for the front door. On the way it occurred to him this could very well be Dolly, and if it was, and she was insistent, it could lead to complications he didn't much care to think about. Thinking about them anyway, he opened the door.

It wasn't Dolly, but it might better have been Dolly. Even Dolly would have been better than Deputy Inspector Callaghan.

11

"OKAY, MUG," SAID DEPUTY Inspector Callaghan, "let's you and me talk."

"Sure," said Engel. "Come on in."

But Callaghan was already in, crossing the foyer toward the living room. Engel shut the door and followed him, saying, "I was just about to leave, you know that? I was on my way down to see you."

Callaghan turned on Engel a fish-eye that made Nick Rovito's look almost pleasant. "I know," he said. "I'm sure of that. That's why I came over, to save you the trouble."

"No trouble, Inspector. You want a drink?"

"Not on duty." Callaghan looked around the room. "Looks like a discount house," he said.

"*I* like it," Engel told him, which was true. Callaghan was just a no-taste cop, but the comment still stung.

Callaghan said, "Yeah." He was still in his uniform, with the yellow brick road on the side. Normally he wore civilian clothes on duty, except for special occasions like parades and funerals. Apparently he'd been in too much of a hurry this time to change. He sighed, now, and took his hat off and tossed it on the sofa, where it couldn't have looked more out of place. "All right," he said. "Let's start the song and dance."

"What song and dance is that?"

"Where you tell me it's all a case of mistaken identity, I must have got you mixed up with some other guy, you weren't near any funeral parlors at all today. Then you come up with the alibi you worked up for yourself, two or three guys you talked to on the phone before I got here."

Engel took great pleasure in being able to say, "If you mean when you and all those other cops chased me out of Merriweather's grief parlor today, that's what I wanted to come down and talk to you about."

Callaghan's jaw very obligingly dropped three feet. "You *admit* it?"

"Well, sure I admit it. And I admit I don't know how I got away either. I ran down that alley and through that door and out the other side and I was halfway down the next block before I realized you weren't chasing me any more."

Callaghan's jaw climbed back up and arranged itself into a smug smile. He was obviously pleased to see that Engel was going to do at least *some* lying; it restored Callaghan's faith in human nature. He said, "So. You didn't bar that door at the end of the alley, eh?"

"Bar the door? What with?"

"And you didn't knock a lot of full oil drums down in the way of the door either, is that it?"

"Oil drums? I thought I heard something fall down behind me, but I didn't look back to see what it was."

"Of course not. And you didn't back a truck into the other end of the alley either, have I got that straight?"

"Back a truck? What truck? Where did I get a truck from?"

Callaghan nodded. "For a minute there," he said, "I thought one of us had gone crazy. But it's all right, you're talking straight again."

"I'll always talk straight to you, Inspector."

"Yeah? Then maybe you'll tell me how come you ran."

"Because you chased me," Engel said. "Anybody'd run, they see a hundred cops chasing them."

"Not if you had a clear conscience."

"That's afterward," Engel told him. "Afterward is when you say to yourself, 'What the hell, I didn't do anything.' But right at the time, all those cops chasing you, a woman says you bumped off her husband, all you do is *run*."

"And I'll tell you why," Callaghan said. "Because you didn't know who that woman was, that's why. You didn't know if she was the wife of somebody you killed or not. You've done at least one killing recently, maybe more, and you let me know it when you ran away."

"Then why didn't I keep on running?"

Callaghan gave him a crooked smile. "Mind if I use your phone? To help answer the question."

"Go ahead."

"Thanks." Callaghan made the word heavily ironic. He went over the phone, dialed, identified himself, asked for someone named Percy, and when Percy came on the wire, said, "Who talked to that Kane woman? Ask him did she ask any questions about Engel, where he lived, who he was, anything like that. Right, I'll hold on."

Engel went over to the wooden-armed chair where the Kane woman had first sat, and waited there with his arms folded and his feet stretched casually out in front of him. So far as he could see he was in the clear with the law, unless Callaghan wanted to make something out of the Merriweather murder, but if he did he surely would have mentioned something about it now. So Engel, incurious, just sat and waited.

Callaghan, after a moderately long silence, said, "Yeah? She did? That's fine." He grinned crookedly over the phone, said so long, hung up, and turned to Engel. "Now I'll answer your question," he said. "You stopped running, and you decided not to set up an alibi for yourself, because the Kane woman came here and told you she'd been to Headquarters to tell her story and get you off the hook."

"She did?"

"Yes, she did. She got your address from one of our boys at Headquarters, because she said she wanted to send you a letter and apologize. But she didn't send you a letter, she came here in person, straight from Headquarters."

"Is that a fact?"

"Yeah, that's a fact." Callaghan pointed toward the bar. "She had a drink while she was here, there's the glass. She probably left just before I got here."

"Fancy that."

Callaghan said, "That's the trouble with you punks, you all think you're smart, smarter than anybody, and all the same you're nothing but stupid. Stupid. You'll die in jail, Engel, and maybe in the chair."

"Will I?"

"Yes, you will." Callaghan pointed a knobby finger at Engel. "You were stupid today," he said. "You let me know there was something to look for. You let me know you've done at least one killing recently. Now I start looking. You think I won't find what I'm looking for?"

"That's what I think, all right," said Engel. "I don't kill people, I'm not the type. I got spooked today, that's all, just the way anybody would in a situation like that."

"I'll get the goods on you, Engel, don't you think I won't. I'll remember that business about the alley a long, long time."

"Why not set me up for the Merriweather killing?" Engel asked him, pushing the subject because he wanted to know why Callaghan hadn't mentioned it.

Callaghan said, "I wish I could, but the timing's off. We know to the minute when Merriweather was killed, and it was before you were even inside the front door. *I'm* your alibi on that killing."

"What do you mean, you know to the minute when he was killed?"

"What do you care for?"

Engel cared because the Merriweather killing was, he was convinced, connected somehow with the missing Charlie Brody and his missing suit, but what he said was, "It's a provocative statement, that's all. You say you know to the minute when he was killed, and it was when you and I were out front, so it's a provocative statement. I've got a natural curiosity about how come you know to the minute when he was killed."

Callaghan said, "He was talking on the phone. He said, 'There's someone at the door, I'll call you back.' Then he broke the connection. The party he was talking to had something to say to him right away, and dialed his number again, and got a busy signal. The reason for that is, when he was stabbed he knocked the phone off his desk and the receiver came off the hook. So he was killed between the time he hung up and the time the fellow he was talking to finished dialing again and got the busy signal, which is about a minute, and this fellow knows what time that minute was because he was late for an appointment and looking at his watch the same time he was dialing."

"Who was he talking to?"

Callaghan frowned. "You ask a lot of questions. Get the habit from talking to cops?"

"You don't have to tell me," Engel said, "I was just curious, that's all, just making conversation."

"It was a fellow named Brock, Kurt Brock. Merriweather's assistant. Merriweather fired him yesterday, or laid him off, I couldn't get it straight which, and Brock was talking to him about coming back to work for him. When Merriweather hung up, Brock thought he was just giving him the brush-off, and he had a date to get to, so that's why he called back right away."

"Giving himself and me alibis," Engel said.

Callaghan said, "Sharp, aren't you? We checked that, and he's alibied from the other end. His landlady knows he was there, and knows when he left. She's one of those landladies knows everything happens on the block."

Engel said, "So I'm in the clear."

"I could make trouble for you if I wanted," Callaghan told him. "Malicious mischief, maybe, or obstructing a policeman in the performance of his duty. You committed about thirty-seven misdemeanors this afternoon, whether you know it or not. But I don't want you on any misdemeanor, that's the easy way out. Get you a fine, maybe thirty days in the Tombs if I'm lucky, you can shrug that off as just the price for a good story you can tell around the bars. No, what I want you on is a felony, a big felony. Something that'll stick, and something that'll get you out of circulation for good. Something like murder one, say, that ought to do the trick."

"Sure," said Engel. "You have a lot of fun." He smiled, free and easy, because he knew for once he was clear and clean and safe. Callaghan would be looking for murders Engel had performed, and murder was just about the only felony Engel *hadn't* performed recently, so there wouldn't be anything out there for Callaghan to find but a wild goose and he was welcome to it.

"I'll be seeing you again," Callaghan said. "Don't leave town, in the meantime, you may be a witness in the Merriweather case."

"Sure. I've got nowhere to go."

"Except Sing Sing."

On that note Deputy Inspector Callaghan left, taking his surly disposition with him. Engel shut the hall door after him and then went back through the living room and deeper into the apartment. In the bedroom he said, softly, "All right, Mrs. Kane, it's safe now. He's gone."

There wasn't any answer.

Engel frowned. He looked in the soundproof room and it was empty. He looked in the bedroom closet and under the bedroom bed. He called, "Mrs. Kane? Mrs. Kane?" He looked in the bathroom and in the sauna (producer), looked in the kitchen, looked everywhere.

Finally he got to the rear door, which let out on a narrow room where the cistern and the service elevator were, where his milk would be delivered if he had milk delivered, and she wasn't there either.

"Well, I'll be damned," he said to himself. "She's gone again."

12

HOW MANY KURT BROCKS could there be? According to Engel's telephone directories, one in Manhattan, none in Queens, two in Brooklyn, none in The Bronx. Total: three.

The Manhattan Kurt Brock was nearest, so Engel went to see him first. He wanted to talk to the Kurt Brock who'd been fired by Merriweather, because he wanted to know how long ago this firing had taken place. If Brock had been fired before Charlie Brody's body arrived at the grief parlor, nothing more was to be said. If he wasn't fired until more recently than that, there was a good chance he might know something Engel could use.

Kurt Brock number one lived on West 24th Street, between Ninth and Tenth avenues. The south side of that block was one long apartment building, London Terrace, which covered the whole area bounded by 23rd and 24th streets and Ninth and Tenth avenues. Brock lived across the street from this monstrosity, in one of a row of identical elderly narrow buildings four stories high, all converted to one- and two-room apartments, each set back a bit from the sidewalk with greenery or concrete in front, depending on the owner's whim. The buildings were all run together in a row, with no space at the sides, in the normal New York manner.

The one Brock lived in had shrubbery and gravel inter-mixed in its front space, in a vaguely Japanese effect spoiled by a heavily European thick iron fence across the front bound-ary. Engel pushed open the gate in this, crossed the slate path to the front door, and was about to step inside when a voice above him called, "Kurt! Kurt, did you remember the liquor store?"

Engel stepped back a pace and looked up. An amiable heavy-set middle-aged woman was looking at him from a second-story window. When she saw his face she stopped smiling, looked baffled for a second, and then said, "Oh, I'm sorry, I thought you were Kurt."

"Kurt Brock?"

"Yes, that's right."

"He's the one I came to see. Isn't he home now?"

"He's gone to the supermarket. Down at the corner. He'll be back soon, why don't you sit down and wait?"

"Thank you."

There was a low bench set against the front of the build-ing, beside the door. Sitting on it, one could look across the shrubbery, over the fence, and out to the sidewalk, the street beyond, and—the normally near horizon of New York—the bulging brick apartment building across the way. Engel sat down there, lit a cigarette, and waited. This might be the wrong Kurt Brock, he might be wasting his time right now, but as long as he was here he might as well check this one off the list. No sense coming back twice if he didn't have to.

He waited ten minutes, and then the gate was pushed open by a tall slender young man with his arms full of grocery-store sacks. He was about Engel's height and slenderness, but looked to be half a dozen years younger, probably in his early twenties. He had black hair, dark piercing Mediterranean eyes, prominent cheekbones, sallow skin. All in all, vaguely decadent good looks, as though he might have once upon a time been a gigolo.

Above Engel's head, the woman called, "Kurt! Did you remember the liquor store?"

"Right here." He waved a smaller brown paper bag held in his right hand, out at the perimeter of the larger grocery sacks. When he smiled up at the woman in the window his face softened, he looked much more pleasant and much less cynically worldly-wise.

"There's a man here to see you," the woman called, presumably pointing down at the top of Engel's head.

The smile vanished at once, and Kurt Brock's face took on such a guarded, wary quality it was almost as though steel plates had been erected all around it. He came forward walking catlike, ready to leap in any direction, the armful of grocery sacks unfortunately spoiling the effect. "You wanted to see me?"

"You're the Kurt Brock who worked for Augustus Merriweather." Engel had begun the sentence as a question, midway through had thought better of it, and had finished it as a direct statement. He instinctively didn't want Brock to see any doubt or indecision in him.

Brock's wariness lessened, replaced by feigned weariness. "You're from the police again, I suppose."

Engel made a head-and-hand motion that might have meant yes.

"I've already made a statement twice," Brock said. "Once on the phone, and once to two patrolmen who came around."

"Red tape," Engel explained, knowing it was an explanation that would satisfy anybody about anything official.

It satisfied Brock, who sighed, shrugged behind the grocery sacks, and said, "Very well. Come along upstairs."

"I'll carry one of those for you."

"Would you? Thanks."

They went into the building and up the stairs, Brock leading the way, Engel following, each carrying a sack of groceries. Brock also carried the smaller package from the liquor store, and stopped at the door to the second-floor front apartment in order to deliver it. There was a delay while the woman thanked Brock, found her purse, paid him for the bottle, and thanked him all over again, while the sack of groceries in Engel's arms steadily put on weight. In the interval, with nothing else to do, he memorized the contents of the sack, as much of them as he could see: celery, English muffins, eggs, raspberry yogurt, tomatoes. Plus cans of this and that down at the bottom of the sack, which he couldn't see but his arms could feel.

Finally the liquor transaction was done and Brock led the way up one more flight, fumbled with his key, and let Engel into a small neat room that somehow didn't look like a place where anyone lived. It had more the appearance of an anteroom or dressing room; a place where one came to rest and prepare for something to be done outside. Perhaps the matador, before going out to meet the bull, would dress and bless himself in a room like this, tucked away beneath the stands. Perhaps the brand-new Presidential candidate, before going out to address the convention, would sit and go over last-minute changes in his speech in a room like this, past a small door behind the platform.

The room was functional, that's why, merely functional. A studio couch which was presumably a bed by night was now covered neatly with zebra-stripe material and two ornamental orange cushions. A neat breakfast set, table and two chairs of formica and tubular chrome and orange seating material, was tucked away against the wall next to a tiny, clean, white, barren kitchenette. The carpet was gray, the curtains orange and white, the rest of the furniture bright and neat and functional and uninteresting, of the kind loosely called Danish Modern but which might with more accuracy be called Motel Standard.

Brock said, "Do you mind if I put these things away while we talk? I have some perishables."

"Go ahead." Engel put his grocery sack on the table, flexed his arms, and said, "As I get it, you were on the phone to Merriweather just before he was killed."

"Yes." Brock opened the refrigerator door and started putting things away. Within the refrigerator his food was lined and stacked as neatly as on any supermarket's shelf. "At least, that's what the police say. I know when I tried to call him back the line was busy."

"Because the phone was knocked off the hook when he was killed, I know." Engel lit a cigarette, thinking carefully. Brock had assumed he was a cop, and that was good because it meant he'd answer questions. But now the problem was to ask the questions a cop might reasonably ask and still get the answers Engel wanted. He tossed his match into a gleaming spotless glass ashtray inscribed *Acapulco Hilton,* and said, "You were calling about your job, is that it?"

"Yes. Getting it back, yes."

"I don't have that part straight. You quit your job, you were laid off, you were fired, what was it?"

Brock finished putting his groceries away and shut the refrigerator door. "I was fired," he said. He grinned sheepishly, and shrugged. "I suppose I deserved it," he said, and folded up the grocery sacks and put them away.

"You were fired when?"

Brock came out of the kitchenette, leaving it as spotless and unused-looking as before he'd gone into it It made Engel vaguely uneasy to be in the presence of a man who traveled with no wake; as though he'd seen a cat walk through mud and leave no tracks. It was somehow ghostly.

Brock said, "Fired yesterday. Why don't you sit down, Mr.—?"

"Engel." When there's no need to lie, don't lie. Engel sat down in a trim lightweight chair with wooden arms and frame, bright-hued foam rubber cushions, and a look of transience, while Brock settled himself gracefully on the zebra-striped studio couch. He was wearing black slacks, somewhat tight, and a lime-green polo shirt.

Engel said, more to himself than Brock, "Fired yesterday . . ." Which meant Brock was still an employee when Charlie Brody had come under Merriweather's care. Engel said, "What were you fired for?"

Brock smiled again, that boyish pleasant grin. "Incompetence," he said, "sheer incompetence. Plus being too often late for work and not taking a sufficiently whole-hearted interest in my profession." The smile broadened, became positively collegiate. "Somehow," he said, "I never could see myself being a mortician the rest of my life."

Nor could Engel. He said, "How did you go to work for him in the first place?"

"I was a chauffeur for a while. I worked for some people on Long Island, until . . ." He shrugged casually. "That's all past, a long story and not related. When I needed another job, I thought I would still drive. I almost went to work for a taxicab company, but then I answered an ad in the *Times* and it turned out to be Mr. Merriweather, looking for someone to drive the hearse."

"Is that what you did, drive the hearse?" Which would be unfortunately removed from any connection with Charlie Brody's body.

"At first. But Mr. Merriweather took an interest in me, and so I suppose did Mrs. Merriweather. At any rate, he was training me to be his assistant, eventually perhaps his partner. So I wound up doing general work for him, just about everything there is to do in a funeral home."

"And then he fired you?"

Brock again combined the smile and shrug. "The more I learned about the business," he said, "the less I was enthralled by it. On the other hand, I wasn't at all ready to leave that employment, which is why I phoned him today, to see if he'd calmed down and would take me back."

"Had he?"

"I didn't have a chance to find out."

All things considered, Engel was willing to guess there was more to the story than Brock had told, and his further guess was that the rest of the story had to do somehow with Mrs. Merrieather. Had Brock been doing a little extracurricular work there? Or had Mrs. Merriweather merely tried too hard to be helpful to Brock with her husband, with or without Brock's request that she do so? It was something like that anyway, and Engel was pleased with himself for figuring it out, but on the other hand, it wasn't getting him any closer to Charlie Brody and that goddam blue suit, so he said, "I'll tell you the truth, Mr. Brock, I don't know a thing about the undertaker business, and now with Mr. Merriweather murdered I've got to do some learning. I've got to know the routine, the methods, what Mr. Merriweather's normal day was like, you see what I mean?" Engel, saying all this, could barely keep a smile of pleasure from spoiling the whole effect. It was just that he was working with his own memory of interviews with cops in order to try to sound like a cop himself, and he was proudly sure he was doing just fine.

Apparently he was. Brock leaned forward in an attitude that declared his desire to help, and said, "Anything I can tell you, Mr. Engel, I'll be glad to."

"I tell you what," said Engel. "Let's take the last body you worked on, you and Mr. Merriweather, you tell me everything that's done from beginning to end."

"Well, not everybody likes that kind of detail, Mr. Engel."

"I don't mind. In my business . . ." Engel let the sentence end with his own smile-shrug combination, then said, "We'll just take the last body you worked on. What would that be?"

"The last client?"

"Client?"

Brock's sudden smile this time was slightly sardonic. "That was Mr. Merriweather's word," he said. "He's a client himself now, isn't he?"

"All right, who was the last client you worked on?"

"That would be the retired policeman, O'Sullivan. He was buried this morning."

Engel covered his disappointment. "Of course," he said. "That was the last one you worked on."

"Of course," said Brock, "I didn't deal with him all the way through, I got fired first, but I could tell you what part I did, and then what Mr. Merriweather did after I left, it's all standard stuff."

"I'd rather," Engel told him, seeing a ray of hope, "you told me about a client you actually worked on all the way through. Who would that be, the one before O'Sullivan?"

"Yes, that would be another man, a Mr. Brody."

"Brody."

"Yes. Heart attack. I think he was a salesman of some kind."

Engel settled more comfortably on the chair, and said, "Fine. Tell me about him."

"Well, it was the widow who called. Some business associate of her husband's had recommended Merriweather, I think. I went out with the pickup car, made the initial arrangements with the widow and met with the doctor, and the pickup team with me put the client in the travel box."

"Travel box," said Engel.

"That's what we call it. Looks pretty much like a regular casket, but with handles coming out of each end, like a stretcher. I think the city boys use a wicker basket, which would be more practical for cleaning and everything, but families might get upset if they saw a client stuffed away in a basket, so we use the travel box."

"Sure," said Engel.

Brock seemed to consider. "Nothing special about the Brody case," he said. "Well, one thing. There'd been an accident of some sort, he was burned rather badly about the head, so there wouldn't be any viewing. Actually, there's the whole area of cosmetology we didn't get into with Brody, maybe I ought to pick a different client to tell you about."

"No, no, that's fine, we've started with this man Whats-is-name—"

"Brody."

"Right, Brody. We've started with him, let's finish with him. Then, if there's anything different you'd do normally, we can go back over it again."

Brock shrugged and said, "If you think that's the way to do it."

"I do."

"Then fine. All right, we brought Brody back and put him in the icebox overnight. In the morning the widow came in—with some friends of her husband's, I think—and they selected the casket, worked out the arrangements; I remember it struck me it was a surprisingly big funeral they were setting up for a little salesman, whatever he was."

"Then what?"

"Then we embalmed him, of course. Or actually we did it the night before."

"Embalmed."

"Yes. We drain the blood out of him, and put the embalming fluid in."

"In the veins."

"And arteries, yes."

Engel was beginning to feel slightly less than well. He said, "Then what?"

"Then of course we clean out the internal organs and—"

"Internal organs."

Brock motioned at his own torso. "Stomach," he said. "All that."

"Oh."

"Then we fill the cavity with cavity fluid and—"

"Cavity?"

Brock made the same motion as before. "Where the internal organs were."

"Oh," said Engel. He lit a cigarette and it tasted like a barn in summer.

"That's all done the night before," said Brock. "When we get the client. Then we wait till the next morning for the restoration."

"That's when Brody's wife came."

"Well, that's what's happening *up*stairs. Downstairs, usually, there's the restoration. Cosmetics, you know, this and that, we make the client look as though he's sleeping. Sew the lips shut, use make-up for any little deformities, any little problems—"

"Yeah, fine, that's fine."

"Of course, with Brody we didn't do all that, because there wasn't a viewing."

"Right."

"We did *some* of course, the normal embalming procedures, but there was hardly any face there to put make-up on, you know. And no lips to sew."

Engel swallowed and put his cigarette out. "Yeah, well, then what?"

"Then we arrange the client in his casket. Well, no, first he goes back in the icebox till the viewing, or the wake, whatever you want to call it. Then we arrange him in the casket and bring him upstairs for the viewing. With Brody there was a wake, but no viewing. Closed casket. He got a pretty big crowd anyway, a lot more than I expected. I can't figure out what he sold, to get that kind of crowd at his wake."

"Who does that part?" Engel asked. "Putting him in the casket, getting him ready for the viewing."

"Well, either Mr. Merriweather or me. Sometimes I'd do the whole job on a client myself, sometimes he would, most times one of us would do one thing and one would do another."

"What about Brody? As an example, I mean."

"Well, I went and got him, had the first discussion with the widow. Then Mr. Merriweather had the second discussion with the widow. I did the embalming, and he arranged the client in the casket and set up the casket in the viewing room."

So Merriweather was still the last one to see Brody dead. Unless . . .

Engel said, "Is there anybody else around when you're doing all this? People drop in to watch or anything?"

"Oh, no." Brock gave the collegiate smile again. "It isn't the sort of operation to draw a crowd," he said. "Besides, it's illegal to have anyone present at the embalming, against the law. Oh, I think members of the family could be there, but they never are."

It was a dead end. Engel got to his feet and said, "Well, thanks. You've been a big help."

"You want a drink before you go?" Brock patted his own trim belly, said, "Something to fill the inner man, eh?"

Cavity fluid. Engel said, "No, thanks," and then, remembering Callaghan, added, "Not on duty."

"Oh, right, forgot about that. Well, if there's anything else, any time at all, I'll be more than glad to help."

"That's fine. Fine."

Brock walked Engel to the door, smiled one last time, and shut the door as Engel walked away down the hall to the stairs.

Going down the stairs, it seemed to Engel he was wasting his time, going at this whole thing the wrong way. Instead of starting with Merriweather, and going through Brock to . . . well, to wherever, instead of doing that he should start at the other end, with Charlie Brody himself. He should talk to Brody's wife, and he should talk to Brody's immediate boss Fred Harwell, and he should talk to anybody else who might have known about the heroin in Brody's suit. Even if Merriweather's murder *were* connected with Charlie Brody's disappearance—and though he still believed it was, because otherwise the coincidence was just too pat, he nevertheless realized coincidence does happen sometimes and he could yet be wrong—but even if there were a connection, he was still going at things the wrong way. He hadn't fully realized it up to now, but now that he'd come to a dead end with Brock, he could see just how he'd been going wrong.

The trouble was, in the game of cops and robbers he just wasn't set up to be a cop. His sympathies, his interests, his training and his inclination were all on the other side. No wonder he was going at things backward, no wonder he was coming to dead ends.

Thinking these things, he came out to the street, looked right and left, and went off to the right, toward Tenth Avenue, which was closer. There he stood, on the corner, waiting for a cab.

It took a few minutes, Tenth Avenue being a bit off the beaten path. He stood there, gradually getting impatient, and finally decided to walk down to Ninth. He'd taken half a dozen paces from the corner when a white open Mercedes-Benz 190SL rolled by, with Margo Kane, the mystery woman, at the wheel. She had replaced her black gown with white stretch pants and a bulky orange sweater, and she was looking so hard for a parking space along the curb that she didn't notice Engel at all.

Of course there were no parking spaces, there never are in New York. Ahead of Engel, on the other side of the street, there was a cleared area along the curb by a fire hydrant, and this is where Margo Kane parked, turning the wheel with casual graceful abandon. She got out of the car—her sandals were lime-green, the same color as Brock's polo shirt—tripped across the street on dancing feet, and went into Brock's building.

Engel stood on the sidewalk, looking toward the doorway into which she had disappeared. "Oh ho," he said. Not that he knew what this new development meant, if anything, not that he could immediately connect it up with the disappearance of Charlie Brody, but just that it was interesting. So interesting, in fact, that he said it a second time: "Oh ho."

13

THERE WAS ANOTHER NOTE from Dolly, printed with lipstick on another résumé and attached with another false fingernail:

> Honey?
> Where are you?
> Dont you want to see me?
> Don't you *remember?*
>
> DOLLY

Engel remembered. He looked at the note sadly, shook his head, took it down from the door, and went into the apartment. He made himself a Scotch and water without the water, sat down by the telephone, and started making his calls.

First to Archie Freihofer, who ran the girl part of the organization. When he got hold of Archie, Engel identified himself and said, "I want to see Charlie Brady's wife."

"What, Bobbi?"

"That's it. Bobbi."

"Al, I'm sorry. We decided, all things considered, the little lady oughta have a few days to herself before she comes back on active duty. It'll be the first of the week before she starts to work, and then to be truthful with you there's a waiting list as long as your arm. A lot of the boys have chosen to decide, it seems to me, to make a really beautiful gesture of affection and respect for Charlie Brody and at the same time see to it a little extra cash against emergencies goes into the little lady's stocking."

There was no interrupting Archie once he got talking. The only thing to do was wait till he decided to stop again, even if only to take a breath. At this point, spying a little bit of silence coming up after the word "stocking," Engel quickly threw some words of his own into the breach, saying, "No, Archie, that isn't what I want. I'm talking about business."

"So what have I been talking about, a game Scrabble?"

"I want to *talk* to Mrs. Brody," Engel said.

Archie said, "Al, she's using her professional name again. Bobbi Bounds."

"Whatever name she's using, I want to talk to her. Official business. You can check with Nick Rovito."

"Check? I take your word for it, what do you think? You want to go see her, or you want her to come see you?"

"I'll go see her. Is she living at the same place where she lived with Brody?"

"No, she's moved in with a couple other girls, you know how they are they like to be with friends that understand the situation, you know?"

"What about the apartment?"

"The old one? Charlie's? I wouldn't know."

"Give me her phone number, Archie. Maybe we can save time, I can meet her at the old apartment."

"Hang on, I'll look it up."

110

Engel hung on. Archie came back a minute later, gave him the number, and Engel thanked him and broke the connection. Then he dialed the number Archie had just given him.

It was answered on the third ring by a female voice harsh with suspicion: "Yeah?"

"Is Bobbi there?"

"Who's calling?"

"Al Engel. I'm calling for Nick Rovito, on urgent business connected with her late husband."

"Hang on."

Again he hung on, and the next voice he heard belonged to Bobbi Bounds, saying, "Mr. Engel?"

"I rode in the car with you yesterday," Engel reminded her. "Up front."

"Yes, sure, I know who you are."

The tone of respect in her voice surprised him, till he remembered just how far down in the pecking order of the organization Charlie Brody had been. The grand send-off had tended to make him forget that.

He said, "Has everything been cleared out of the old apartment yet?"

"No, not yet. I've taken some of my own things, but Charlie's stuff is still all there."

"I want to meet you there, this afternoon. Are you free?"

"Sure, I guess so."

Engel looked at his watch and it was four-thirty. "At six o'clock," he said.

"Is there something wrong, Mr. Engel?"

"Not exactly. A little problem we got to get straightened out, that's all."

"I'll be there."

"Fine."

Next, Fred Harwell, who was in his office. Engel said, "Fred, has Nick told you the latest development?"

"Which latest development is that?"

"About Charlie Brody's suit."

"The last I heard about that was at the meeting, when Nick told you go dig it up. About which, Al, you know you could do me a big favor if you'd talk to Nick about that, how it wasn't really my fault about not remembering the suit. I mean, nobody—"

"Fred, I—"

"Wait a second, Al, this is important. Because *nobody* remembered that suit, Al, not just me, *nobody*. Al, if you could—"

"Fred, will you—?"

"You're closer to him than anybody, Al. If you could just put in a good word for me, explain about how—"

"I will," Engel said, just to shut him up.

"It could have happened to anybody," said Fred, who apparently hadn't heard him, or couldn't adapt to Engel's having agreed so easily.

"Right," Engel said. "I'll talk to him."

"You will?"

"I will. If you'll shut—"

"I appreciate that, Al."

"Yeah. If you'll shut up and let me talk to *you*, I'll talk to him. If not, the hell with you."

"Al, I'm sorry. I didn't mean to monopolize the conversation."

"Yeah, well—"

"It's just been preying on my mind, that's all. Nick hasn't said anything to me since then, but I know—"

"Shut up, Fred."

"What?"

"I said shut up, Fred."

Engel really didn't believe the silence that followed, and it stretched for maybe ten seconds before he understood that Fred had shut up and it was now possible to talk. When he got that straight he said, "I want to ask you about Charlie, Fred, because we don't have the suit yet, and we don't have the suit yet because we buried an empty coffin yesterday."

"We bur—Oh, I'm sorry."

"Yeah. Now, Nick's given me the job of finding out where the suit *is* now, which means find out where the body is now, which means find out who took him, and how they took him, and why they took him. But mostly who. I found out how, because the undertaker was bumped off today and—"

"Bump—! Oops, sorry. I'll keep quiet."

"Yeah. The way I figure it, the undertaker was in on the snatch, and whoever did it with him killed him to keep him from talking, or something like that. So that's how it was done, but that still leaves who and why. Now, you knew Charlie Brody, so maybe you can tell me who'd steal his dead body and why."

"What? Why would I—? Uhh, are you done?"

"I'm done."

"Okay. So how would I know—I mean, why would anybody want to steal a dead body? Except the heroin, maybe."

"You'd have to know the heroin was in the suit, and you'd have to know the suit was on the body. Who'd know both of those things?"

"I really don't know, Al. I guess the wife knew he was wearing the suit—isn't she the one gave it to the undertaker?"

"It wouldn't have been her," said Engel. "She wouldn't have to—"

"I'm not suggesting it was."

"Yeah. She wouldn't have to steal the body to get the suit back. All she'd have to do was bury him in some other suit."

"Well," said Fred, "there's no reason to take the whole body if all you want's the suit. I mean, what are you going to do with the body later? After you get the snow out of the suit?"

Engel said, "You know, I been thinking something like that. Maybe whoever swiped Charlie didn't have anything to do with the heroin in the suit, maybe he didn't even know it was there."

"That makes a lot more sense," said Fred.

"Nothing makes sense," Engel told him. "Maybe I'll call you back."

"You won't forget to talk to Nick."

"I won't forget," Engel promised, and hung up, and forgot.

His drink was gone, so he went over and made another, and stayed leaning against the bar, trying to figure things out.

Why steal a dead body?

Not to experiment on, they didn't do that kind of thing any more. People gave themselves to science in their wills and like that.

And not to get the heroin in the suit the dead body was wearing either—which was the mistaken assumption Engel'd been making all along—because it would be simpler just to take the suit.

No, whoever had stolen Charlie Brody had done it because he wanted Charlie Brody. Or at least Charlie Brody's body.

Why would anybody want Charlie Brody's body?

Engel looked in his glass and saw to his surprise that somehow or other it had become empty again. He corrected that, and while he was doing so the phone rang. He went over, carrying the fresh drink, picked up the receiver and said, "Hello."

"Aloysius, I'm sorry to disturb you, and I won't keep you long, and I wouldn't have called at all if it wasn't important, you know I wouldn't."

"What?"

"I know you can't come to dinner tonight, Aloysius," she said, "but what I want to know is, can you come tomorrow night? I have to know before I go to the store. I wouldn't bother you—"

"That's why you called?"

"I don't want to take up your—"

"The answer is no," said Engel, and hung up. He stood there a minute or two, next to the phone, and contemplated the fact that sooner or later he was going to have to be unkind to his mother. There was no getting around it, no getting around it. Sooner, or later. Sooner, or later.

The phone rang.

Sooner.

He picked up the receiver. Into it he said, "California."

A young female voice said, "Impossible. I didn't dial the area code."

"What?"

"You can't get California unless you dial the area code. Every place has an area code, and the *only* way to get that place is *dial* the area code. Since I didn't dial the area code you can't possibly be California. You must be New York."

A little dazed, Engel said, "That's right. I'm New York."

"Are you Mr. *Engel* New York?"

"I think so."

"Well, this is Margo Kane again. I hope I'm not interrupting anything?"

"No, no. Not a thing."

"I've been thinking," she said, "about all the inconvenience I caused you today, and really my conscience is bothering me something awful."

"Think nothing of it," Engel told her.

"No, really, I mean it. If you aren't doing anything, I'd like very much to buy you a dinner tonight. May I?"

"You don't need to," Engel said. "We're square."

"No, I insist. It's the least I can do. What time should I pick you up?"

Engel was getting glimmers. He said, "Well, I have an appointment at six, I ought to be back by seven, then I'll have to change."

"This isn't crowding your evening too much, is it? We can make it just as late as you like."

"Eight," Engel said.

"You're sure of that? That's not rushing you too much?"

"No, that's fine."

"It really does have to be tonight, or not for days and days. Tomorrow night is poor Murray's wake, and then the next day the funeral and all, and I probably won't eat a thing all day after that. So, if it isn't too much, tonight's by far the best for me."

"It's fine with me, too."

"Besides, I am looking forward to seeing you again. And that delicious apartment of yours."

"Yeah, that's right."

"At eight, then."

"Right."

Engel hung up, and tasted his drink, and grinned to himself because for one of the few times all day he knew what was going on. Mrs. Kane had gone to see Brock, who told her about the policeman who'd just been there to see him. Engel had given his right name, which Brock must have mentioned, and Mrs. Kane immediately had known who it was and that it wasn't a cop. So now she wanted to know what Engel was up to, and hoped to find out over dinner.

Because of Brock? Sure, because of Brock and the inheritance she expected from her husband. She and Brock probably had a thing going, maybe for a long time now and maybe brand-new, and she wanted to know if Engel was going to cause any trouble.

Then Engel once more said, "Oh ho," because another thought had come to him. Maybe Brock had been fired because Merriweather had caught him fooling around with Mrs. Kane, with one of the customers. That made sense, and the timing was right on it. Brock and the widow off in a corner behind some flowers for a little slap and tickle, Merriweather happens by, he's shocked, he's outraged, he blames Brock for the whole thing and fires him on the spot.

All of which was, Engel admitted himself, brilliant deduction on his part and not a damn bit of help in finding Charlie Brody.

"Oh, Charlie," Engel said aloud, the words full of weariness, "where the hell are you? Where are you, Charlie, where the hell have you got to?"

14

WHERE CHARLIE BRODY RESIDED in death was any-body's guess at the moment, but where he had resided in life was both known and normal. He and his missus had shared an apartment on Manhattan's West Side, on 71st Street near West End Avenue, where Brody had blended with his neighbors the way a black cat blends with a coal mine. It was a neighborhood full of mild-mannered middle-aged men with thinning hair and weak eyes, white-collar workers in the lower echelons of huge corporations, and this description—until his death—had fitted Charlie Brody to a T.

His apartment, too, looked like any other apartment in the area, respectable if somewhat seedy, predictable and staid. An imitation Persian carpet lay on the living-room floor. A bulky sofa and two chairs, one of which matched the upholstery of the sofa, were arranged about the room exactly as they would have been arranged by any other family in the neighborhood. The television set—a console, with an unused phonograph on the right and seldom-used radio on the left—faced the sofa. Lamps, tables, all appropriate and all predictably situated. On the wall above the sofa was a painting of a dirt road in the woods in autumn, with the trees all orange and gold; it might have been a jigsaw puzzle except for the absence of little lines where the pieces were joined.

Bobbi Bounds, the former Mrs. Brody, sat in the middle of all this, quietly weeping. When Engel came in she said, in a small voice, "I'm sorry, Mr. Engel, but I just can't help it. This place is so full of memories."

Which only meant that no matter how typical a thing is, it is still somehow individual.

"I won't take long, Mrs. Brody," Engel promised. "I'd just like to take a quick look through Charlie's papers or whatever."

"He kept a little desk in the bedroom," she said. "You're welcome to look. I haven't touched a thing yet, I just didn't have the heart."

"I'll be as quick as I can."

The bedroom was the inevitable encore to the living room, with the addition of a small roll-top desk in the corner by the closet with the mirror on its door. Engel sat down at this desk, rolled up the top, which hadn't been locked, and spent the next fifteen minutes going through the papers stuffed in the drawers and pigeonholes.

Nothing. Bills, ads clipped out of newspapers, old rent and utility receipts, some travel brochures, income tax records, personal letters, all sorts of junk, but not a thing that helped Engel figure out where Brody was now or why he was there.

The problem was, he couldn't begin to imagine why anybody wanted Brody's body in the first place. If only he could figure out a *reason,* maybe he could get somewhere. But there wasn't anything in the contents of this desk to give him a reason, or even a hint of a reason.

He went through the dresser drawers, too, as long as he was there, and the pockets of the clothing in the closet, and gradually searched the whole room, and still found nothing.

Back in the living room, the widow had stopped her weeping and was sitting now with a soft and resigned stillness. Engel told her, "There's a couple of things I'd like to talk to you about. Why don't we go out and have a drink? Better to talk in a bar."

"Thank you, Mr. Engel. You're a very kind man."

"Think nothing of it."

Mrs. Brody switched off all the lights and carefully locked the door after them. They went downstairs and out to the street and up to 72nd Street, which was the nearest business district. In a Chinese restaurant-plus-bar called The Good Earth they sat at a table, ordered only drinks to the disgust of the scrutable Oriental who served them, and then Mrs. Brody said, "I hope you found what you were looking for, Mr. Engel."

"Well, I'm not sure. Every little bit helps, you know."

"Oh, yes, of course."

He reflected that neither of them knew what he was talking about, and on that reflection allowed the silence to stretch between them.

The problem was, what sort of question could he ask her? She didn't know her husband's body was missing, and Engel didn't have the heart to give her the news. Also, there was no reason to tell her. But what could she know about why it might be taken, or by whom?

The questions that came to his mind were all the wrong kind. He couldn't ask if Charlie had any enemies, because an enemy is something you have before you kick off, not after. So what then?

Following an obscure line of thought, he said, "Did your husband belong to any, uh, groups, Mrs. Brody? You know, fraternal organizations and like that."

"Fraternal—?" The way she looked at him, she had no idea what a fraternal organization was.

Sometimes a high school education got in the way of full communication with the sort of individual one had to deal with in this world. Engel said, "Like the Masons or the Elks or the Rotarians and like that. Or the American Legion, the VFW. Maybe the John Birch Society. I don't know, just groups."

"Oh, no," she said. "Charlie wasn't a joiner. He was very proud of that, not being a joiner. Every once in a while somebody would come around, join this committee, join that group, fight this, demand that, you know the kind of thing you get, and Charlie always use to say, 'Not me, thanks, I'm no joiner.' It used to make them so mad they could spit."

"What about religion?" Engel asked her. "What religion was he?"

"Well, I'm not sure," she said. "He was brought up some sort of Protestant, I guess Methodist. But he wasn't actively in the church at all. I mean, for instance, we had a civil ceremony. In Las Vegas, in one of the marriage chapels there. It was really very beautiful."

She looked as though she were going to start crying again in a second, but instead she dipped her nose into her drink.

Engel said, "He never joined any kind of religious group?"

"No. Not a one. He wasn't a joiner, you know?"

Engel knew. But he'd been hoping, he'd been hoping. He'd all of a sudden gotten this wild idea about a crazy religious cult, Druids or something, and when one of their number died they took the body themselves and had some special thing they did with it. He knew it was far-fetched, but if it turned out to be so, then it didn't matter how far-fetched it was.

Except it wasn't so.

And Engel had run dry. He kept the conversation going as best he could, but he was stuck and he knew it. He only stayed for the one drink, and then took a cab back downtown to get ready for dinner with Mrs. Kane.

Life was just one damn widow after another.

15

ANOTHER NOTE:

> Are you going to *phone*
> me, or aren't you?
> If you don't want to
> see me any more, just
> *say* so.
> I can take a hint.

It wasn't signed, but it was on a résumé again, in lipstick again, and attached to the door with a false fingernail again, so Engel had a pretty good idea who it was from.

"Life is cruel," he said aloud. He took the note down and went into the apartment.

It was ten after seven, and he spent the next forty-five minutes showering, changing, and generally getting ready for his evening with Mrs. Kane. After all, he told himself, she was at the funeral parlor today, and she knows Kurt Brock, and Kurt Brock was the next to the last one to see Charlie Brody, so I can look at it like I'm still working. There *could* be some connection between Margo Kane and Charlie Brody's body.

There could? Engel, adjusting his tie before the one-way mirror (producer), looked himself in the eye and made a face at himself. What would a woman like Margo Kane want with a body like Charlie Brody?

Well, he told himself defensively, you never knew. That's all, you just never knew.

Sure.

She arrived punctually at eight, coming in smiling and effervescent, wearing now a forest-green knit dress in which she looked almost—but not quite—too thin to be interesting. Her lipstick and nail polish were a less violent shade than before, and her raven-black hair hung in soft folds now around her face.

She came in saying, "I would have insisted on meeting you again if only to see your apartment once more. It's just the most fascinating place I've ever been in."

Engel felt his hackles beginning just slightly to rise. He didn't know exactly why, but he had the feeling there was somehow a touch of mockery in her references to his apartment He said, "I'm ready to go if you are. Or," belatedly, "do you want a drink first?"

She seemed surprised, whether by his tone or his offer he couldn't tell. "We don't have to," she said. "We could have a drink at the restaurant."

"Okay. Fine."

They didn't speak again until they were down in her car, the Mercedes-Benz sports car again, the top still down, once again parked in front of a fire hydrant. Then Engel said, "Don't you ever get tickets, parking like this?"

"You mean those little green cards people put under the windshield wiper?" She laughed, and started the engine. "I have a drawer at home full of those," she said, and pulled away from the curb.

She was a good driver, if a little too competitive. She jockeyed the Mercedes through the narrow Village streets, occasionally leaving shouters and fist-shakers in her wake, and eventually found a ramp up to the West Side Highway, heading north. Comfortably settled in the middle lane, she glanced at Engel and said, "You seem somehow withdrawn tonight. As though you had a rough day."

"Yeah, that's what I did all right. I had a rough day."

"Gangster business?"

The phrase was meant to make him laugh, and he did. "Gangster business," he said. "I'm looking for something that belongs to my boss."

"Something stolen?"

"Lost, strayed, or stolen. I'll tell you when I find it."

"Was that why you were at the funeral parlor today? Looking for it there?"

Engel decided not to give her any sort of specific answer. A simple lie—that he'd been there to pay the Brody bill, for instance—would have ended the matter there and then, but he knew she meant to pump him for his reason for seeing Kurt Brock and it amused him to play it dumb but cozy, make her work for her misinformation. So he said, "Not really. I have all kinds of gangster business."

"Oh, then it *was* gangster business that brought you there."

"I wouldn't say that. Listen, it's too nice a night to talk about funeral parlors."

"Of course," she said, but she couldn't hide the disappointment in her voice.

It was now fully night, a beautiful spring night in the only time of the year when New York City is habitable. At no other time is the air clear, is the sky clean, do the streets and buildings give any indication of personality and color beneath the all-embracing grime. Speeding up the West Side Highway, elevated above the crasser level of the truck-bound streets, the city on their right and the Hudson River and Jersey shore on their left, they were as close as human beings can get to the setting of a thirties movie musical.

There were, naturally, huge billboards boosting beer and trucking companies lining the route on their right, interrupting the view of the city, and across the river, in red neon letters quite large enough to be read from here, blinking slowly on and off, was the one word: SPRY. Women in passing automobiles, caught up in a drifting romantic dream, on seeing that word in the middle of the panorama of night, turned to their husbands and, "Remind me from now on," they said, "to use Crisco."

Mrs. Kane tried no longer on the drive to get information out of Engel. They talked casually, comfortably, about the weather and the city and the driving and other impersonal subjects, and when the silences came between topics they let them come without worrying about them.

At 72nd Street the West Side Highway became the Henry Hudson Parkway. No longer an elevated highway, it raced now amid landscaped greenery, bulky elderly apartment houses on their right. Ahead, gleaming across the river with all its lights, was the George Washington Bridge.

Engel had no idea where Mrs. Kane was taking him, and he didn't worry about it. He sat back in the good car and relaxed. No more did he try to kid himself that he was working. He'd stopped working for today. Tomorrow was soon enough to worry some more about Charlie Brody.

At the bridge they left Henry Hudson and his Parkway, joined the Cross-Bronx Expressway for an elevated trip through some of the less attractive purlieus of New York, thence to the Hutchinson River Parkway north out of the city and out of the state. At the Connecticut line the name changed to Merritt Parkway, and at that point Engel said, "Where we going?"

"A little place I know. Not much farther."

"We have to drive back, too, you know."

She glanced at him again, amused. "Do gangsters have to get up early in the morning?"

"That depends."

They left the Parkway at the Long Ridge Road exit, and drove north a few miles farther before at last she turned off the road and into the parking lot next to a one-time barn now converted into a restaurant called The Turkey Run.

Inside, The Turkey Run was determinedly rustic. Everything was wood, and none of it was smooth. Enough carriage wheels were suspended from the ceiling or hung on the walls or used as room dividers to keep the Conestoga Company in stock for a month. If the lamps on the walls and on the tables didn't look like kerosene lamps it wasn't the designer's fault.

There would be, the mustachioed and absurdly-French waiter told them, a short wait for a table. Would they prefer to wait at the bar?

They would. Over a Scotch sour, Mrs. Kane became moody. "Murray and I used to come here so often," she said. "It's hard to believe we'll never come here again. All that's behind me now, that way of life."

"It must have been a shock," Engel said, because you had to say something in response to a line like that.

"And so—so silly," she said. "So unnecessary."

"Do you want to talk about it?"

She smiled at him, a little crookedly, and rested her hand on his forearm. "You're sweet," she said. "And yes I do. I've had no one to talk to, no one. I've had to keep it all bottled up inside."

"That's no good," Engel said. He found himself thinking how different this one would be from Dolly, contrasting in imagination their individual styles and responses, and forced his mind away at once from such conjectures. That was pretty low of him, he thought, all things considered.

"Murray was a garment manufacturer," she said. "In negligees."

"Uh huh."

"Evening Mist Negligees? You don't know the brand name?"

Engel shook his head. "Sorry."

"Well, of course, women would be more likely to know it."

"Sure."

"That's how I met him. I was a model, and we met at a style show. At first I thought—well, the things people say about the garment business are all true, but—but Murray was different. So sweet, so attentive, so *sincere*. We were married in seven weeks, and I never regretted it, not for a minute. Of course, there was the age difference, but that didn't bother us. How could it? We were in love."

Engel said, "Uh huh," and pulled at his drink.

Mrs. Kane also worked a bit at her Scotch sour. "We had an apartment in town," she said, "and a place in the country. Not far from here, near Hunting Ridge. That's how I happen to know this restaurant, we used to come here so often, so often. And then, of course, Murray had his business, in a loft on West 37th treet. That's where it happened."

"Mm hmm?"

"Murray—well, Murray was more than just a businessman. He'd started in the trade as a designer, and he still did many of his own designs for Evening Mist. He liked very often to stay in the plant in the evenings, alone, after everyone else had gone, and work in his office." She closed her eyes. "I can just see him there, the big fluorescent light on over his head, he bent over his desk, the rest of the loft dark and silent, the bolts of cloth stacked up everywhere." Abruptly again she opened her eyes. "The way the Fire Department reconstructed it," she said, "some of the wiring had become frayed and dangerous. It was such an old building. All at once there was a short-circuit, a fire. All that delicate flimsy cloth, bolt after bolt of it, the fire just swept through it. Of course the sprinklers went on, but they weren't enough. The rest of the building survived, but the interior of the loft was burned to a crisp."

Engel reached out and took her hand, and found it cold. "If you don't want to—"

"But I do, I do. Murray was cut off, you see, from both doors. Being in his own little cubicle, separated from the rest of the floor, it protected him a little, but not enough. In that heat, in all that flame—"

Engel said, "Easy. Easy."

She stopped, held her breath, then let it out in a long sigh. "That's over," she said. "I'm sorry I used you this—"

"Think nothing of it."

"You're very sweet, and I am sorry, but I had to say it, I had to talk about it just once. Now it's done, and I'll never speak of it again." She smiled bravely, and picked up her drink. "To the future," she said.

"To the future."

They got their table shortly after that, and she was true to her word. They talked no more about the late Murray, and concerned themselves once again with lighter and less personal topics. Once when Engel called her Mrs. Kane she insisted that from now on he call her Margo, which after that he did. From time to time she tried to find out gently what he'd been up to at the funeral parlor, but Engel continued for the fun of it to evade her questions. And while she was away to the powder room, he found himself thinking of her in Dolly-like terms once again, and once again he shoved such thoughts down and nailed the lid.

The drive back to the city was as pleasant as the drive up. She drove Engel to his door, and as they shook hands in the car and thanked one another for a lovely evening, it seemed to Engel for one fleet second she expected him to kiss her, but he put the idea down to too much night air and too much Scotch.

She did say, "May I come again to see your apartment? All of it this time."

"Whenever you want," he said.

"I'll call you."

He got out of the car, and she waved and drove away.

Upstairs, he was disappointed to see no note on the door. Had Dolly given up on him? Maybe he shouldn't have wasted tonight after all, maybe he should have been hard at work clearing up the problem at hand.

Well. Tomorrow.

He unlocked the door and went into his apartment and the lights were on. While he was still reacting to that, two of the boys came walking into view, their hands suspiciously close to their jacket lapels. Engel recognized them as organization muscle, but he didn't recognize the expression on their faces and couldn't figure out what they were doing here like this.

Then one of them said, "Nick Rovito wants to see you, Engel."

"Yeah," said the other one. "He wants to see you in a hurry."

Engel looked from one of them to the other. Was this any way to get a message from Nick Rovito? Did this make any sense?

There was only one way a scene like this did make sense, and that way was something Engel didn't even want to think about.

"Come on, Engel," said the first one, moving closer and taking Engel by the elbow. "Let's us go for a little ride."

16

ENGEL HAD SEEN THAT Chevrolet before. But the last time he'd been driving the damn thing, and this time he was put in the back seat to play passenger. One of the messengers got in with him, his hand staying warily near his jacket lapel. The other one got behind the wheel.

The boy at the wheel was named Gittel and the one next to Engel in back was called Fox. They were good professional muscle, constantly on loan to Pittsburgh or Seattle or Detroit, and Engel had known them both for years.

Gittel started the car and it stalled and he said several things. Engel said, "It's standard shift. I was just driving this car last night."

"Shut up," said Fox conversationally.

Gittel, starting the car again, said through clenched teeth, "When we're done with Engel, I'm goin round a little bit with that bastard Kenny."

"He couldn't do any better for me either," said Engel. "It isn't his fault."

"Shut up," Fox offered, "or I'll break your head."

Engel looked at him. "I thought I was your friend."

"I got a dog instead."

133

Gittel had the car going again. He pulled it cautiously away from the curb and headed uptown, in first.

Engel said to Fox, "Can I tell him he oughta shift gears?"

"That's it," said Gittel. "That's all I can take." He pulled the car to the curb again, barely two blocks from Engel's apartment.

Fox said, "Hey! You outa your mind? We're suppose to take him to Nick Rovito first. Besides, you call this a safe place?"

Gittel got out of the car, opened the back door next to Engel, and said, "Out, you son of a bitch."

Engel got out, slowly, looking for a chance.

Gittel shoved the car keys in his hand. "You're so smart," he said, "*you* drive the damn thing."

Engel looked at the keys. Behind him, Fox was saying, "Gittel, that ain't the way it's done! The *mark* don't drive the car!"

"Shut up," Gittel told him, "or *you* get it." To Engel he said, "Get behind the wheel. We'll both be in the back seat, and you oughta know better than try something funny."

"Not anyway till I see Nick," Engel said. "Where you supposed to take me?"

"The mission."

"Right."

They all got back in the car, Engel behind the wheel this time, and once more headed north. Engel by this time was somewhat used to the car, and all the way uptown he only stalled it twice.

The mission was on East 107th Street, in an old store front that had housed a tiny Jewish tailor until some of the neighborhood children had set fire to him. The owner had had a tough time finding another businessman to take the place over, and had been glad finally to rent it to the Jesus Loves You Mission,

Incorporated, one of those fringe organizations that specialize in giving hot soup and mismatched shoes to alcoholics. Since this was one of the blocks where people started throwing bottles, garbage, furniture and each other out the windows at the mere sight of a cop, one of the blocks where the rat population exceeded the human and the rats kept it that way by constantly biting babies, one of the blocks the social workers just didn't want to discuss, there was nothing unusual about a store-front mission opening up there. In fact, not even the owner of the building knew the Jesus Loves You Mission, Incorporated, was a front for the organization.

What safer place could there be in a slum for the neighborhood narcotics peddler than the hot-soup counter at a mission? Customers didn't even have to go home to shoot up. And since the mission had a dormitory upstairs like any other mission, the customers didn't have to go home *after* they shot up either.

Engel parked across the street from this mission now, and he and Gittel and Fox got out of the car. They crossed the rubbish-strewn street, Engel in the middle, and went into the mission.

The front windows of the mission had been whitewashed, and the name of the joint had been put on them in red-painted and very shaky lettering. A notice on the front door—grease pencil on a shirt cardboard—informed the public, with many misspellings, that organ recitals and hymn-singings took place every Friday and Saturday evening at ten o'clock. All welcome.

A half-dozen tottering brittle-boned winos had been clustered outside the door, looking like those who'd been called but not chosen, and at least two dozen more of the same were sprawled around on folding chairs within, in the long main meeting room just inside the door. Religious mottoes were everywhere along the walls, and at the far end, on a slightly raised platform, stood a podium and a small electric organ.

Aside from being an organization front, this place was also a legitimate mission, having as much hot soup and as many mismatched shoes as any other mission in New York, and counters to dispense these items were along the left wall. Juvenile delinquents, looking dangerously bored, manned these posts with less than apparent devotion.

At the far end of the room, near the organ, was a battered brown door with gold lettering on it seemingly done by the same shaky hand that had identified the front windows in red. The lettering announced:

OFFICE
Knock Before Entering

Gittel pushed this door open and entered without knocking. Engel followed him and Fox brought up the rear. Their passage through the meeting room had caused no stir of interest or curiosity, the clientele of missions not normally being of the nosy-parker type.

The office they now entered was a cramped and sloppy room full of second-hand office furniture, on nearly all of which were cardboard cartons stuffed with double-breasted blue pin-stripe suits of a style that even Dennis O'Keefe has stopped wearing. A flabby scabby sloppy type in white religious collar, black clerical suit and red alcoholic nose sat at the desk, adding up numbers on a sheet of yellow paper, doing his work with a thick blunt stub of pencil. He had mud on his shoes, dust on his suit, dandruff on his shoulders, and he ran this joint. "It doesn't matter," he'd been heard to say, "where the support of my mission comes from, or what other uses it may be put to. Crime may produce the money, but the money is used for the Lord's work, and nothing else can have meaning." Most of the time, except for those rare intervals when he was cold sober, he believed what he said, and he made a far better operator of the mission than any cynic from the organization could have done. Nothing cons like sincerity. This fool's name was Clabber, and he liked to be called Reverend.

Not Engel nor either of the other two called him Reverend or anything else at the moment. He looked up from his figuring, bleary-eyed, and watched them pass through, across his cluttered sanctum and through the door on the other side into a room painted black.

All black. Walls and ceiling, black paint on soundproofing. Floor, black linoleum. A black wooden kitchen table and four black kitchen chairs stood in the middle of the room, under a ceiling fixture with three bare twenty-five-watt bulbs in it. A man could scream at the walls and bleed on the floor in here, and none of it would make any difference.

Nick Rovito was sitting at the table, and so was another guy, a humble, hangdog, fiftyish loser with a worried face and bad posture. He looked up at Engel, and then quickly away again. He looked like the kind of natural loser who runs a business, goes bankrupt, sets fire to the store for the insurance and manages only to burn himself up.

Nick Rovito pointed at Engel. "Is that him?"

"Yuh."

"Look at him. Be sure."

The little guy looked at Engel, his eyes pleading as though he and not Engel were the one on the spot. Looking at him, thinking of business and fires, Engel wondered if Murray Kane could possibly have looked like this, but the answer had to be no. Something like this attached to a woman like Margo Kane? Impossible.

Also irrelevant. There were more immediate things to think about, like Nick Rovito saying, "Look at him. Look at his face. Is it him, or are you wasting my time?"

"It's him."

"All right."

Engel said, "What is this, Nick?"

Nick Rovito got up from his seat at the table, came around, and slapped Engel across the face. "I treated you," he said, "like my own son. Better."

"I don't rate this," Engel told him. He knew he was in deeper trouble than he'd ever been in his life before, and he didn't know why, but he had sense enough to keep his head and try for the reasonable approach. Nick Rovito's slap had stung, but that was nothing.

Nick Rovito was saying to the little guy, "All right, that's all. Go home. Tell your friends it's taken care of, and other than that keep your trap shut."

The little guy seemed to get *down* from the chair. He was closed in on himself like a spider that's been poked with a pencil. He scuttled toward the door, blinking, licking his lips, not looking at Engel or anyone.

When he was gone, Engel said, "I don't know what your grievance is, Nick. And I never saw that guy before in my life."

"You will never mention my name again," Nick Rovito said. "I will never mention yours. I wanted you brought here, you greedy little punk, because I wanted to say good-bye. Good-bye."

"You got to tell me what you think I did," Engel said. "I been a help to you for four years, I rate a fair shake from you now."

Nick Rovito stepped back, frowning, squinting. "You never give up," he said. "Or is there more than one thing I could have you on, and you don't know which it is? Is that it?"

"I never did anything to you, Nick," Engel said. "Not once."

The second slap was harder than the first, because it was backhand. "I told you never to mention my name again."

Engel sucked blood in from the corner of his mouth. "I been square with you," he said.

"Tell me one thing," Nick Rovito said. "Did you find the suit? Did you find it and keep it to yourself? That's the kind of thing you'd do, isn't it?"

Engel said, "One of us is crazy," and that earned him the closed fist. He moved his head enough to catch it on the cheekbone instead of the nose.

Fox said, "Nick, please don't mark him. We still got to transport him."

Nick Rovito stepped back again, massaging his knuckles. "You're right. I shouldn't lose my temper with him."

Engel said, "Just tell me what you think I did. I deserve that much."

"Why waste your time, you punk? You don't convince me, so drop it"

"All I ask is tell me in words what I did."

Nick Rovito shook his head. "You just keep trying," he said. "That's one of the things I always liked about you, how you just kept trying. You want me to say it in words? Even though that guy Whatsisname, Rose, that guy Rose was here, you still think there's a chance I mean something else, something you can weasel out of. All right, punk, you want it in words, I'll say it in words."

Engel waited, listening harder than he'd ever listened before in his life.

"You used my name," Nick Rovito said. "You used your connection with me. You went to businessmen, legitimate businessmen like this guy Rose, and you held them up. 'I'm Al Engel,' you said. 'I work with Nick Rovito, and you know who he is. You pay up to me, or I see to it you start getting trouble. Union trouble. Racket trouble. Cop trouble. All sorts trouble.' That's what you told them, you rotten greedy bastard. You worked your own racket inside the organisation."

Engel shook his head. "I never," he said. He knew how serious a thing that was, to use the threat of the organization for personal advantage. There was nothing you could do more serious than that except try to overthrow Nick Rovito himself. An organization can't survive if the members are all trying to be boss, and it can't survive if the members are all out for themselves all the time. So what he was being charged with was enough to make the sweat break out on his forehead and his hands start trembling at his sides.

Nick Rovito said, "I didn't bring you here to listen to you lie."

Engel said, "I wouldn't do such a thing, Ni—I wouldn't. I never saw that guy Rose before in my life."

Nick Rovito shook his head. "Then why would he say it? Why would he accuse you? Why would he identify you? If you never saw him before, if he doesn't know you, why should he take the chance?"

"I don't know. All I know is I never been less than a hundred per cent with you, and you'll know that some day."

Fox laughed, and Gittel motioned like he was playing a violin.

Engel said, "I'm loyal to the end. Callaghan's watching me, he'll want to know where I am. He'll make things hot."

Nick Rovito grinned and shook his head. "Not if you're a killer. Cops don't waste time at all trying to find out who bumped off a killer. And as of tonight you're a killer."

"I am?"

"You went out with a gun tonight, and you killed a punk name of Willy Menchik. Over in Jersey, as he came out of the Bowlorama. You shot him, and then you dropped the gun when you ran away. The cops have it by now, and they'll find your fingerprints all over it."

More and more Engel was convinced he was dreaming. "My prints?"

"You might call me a string saver," Nick Rovito said. "I never throw anything away. Like the gun you used on Conelly?"

"You kept it?"

"A nice set of prints, kept fresh in cold storage. By morning Callaghan will be looking for you with a warrant on murder one. By tomorrow night hell find you, rubbed out. No witnesses, no questions, no evidence. No need to waste time and money on a trial for you. Hell wash his hands and go think about something else."

It was true. Engel shook his head, trying to rid himself of the notion, trying to make the last half-hour go away and not have happened, but it did no good.

Nick Rovito gave him a mock salute. "Good-bye, you punk," he said. "Good-bye, you second-rate cheap bastard."

"Nick—"

"Take him out of here."

Gittel and Fox closed in, getting him by the arms just above the elbow, squeezing hard, in a grip he'd used himself more times than he could count. They took him out of the black room and through the office with its blinking fool and through the main meeting room and out to the street and across to the car.

The hubcaps were all gone. So was the radio antenna. So was the glass from the taillights. The glove compartment had been rifled and the rear seat had been slashed with a knife.

Gittel looked this way and that along the quiet street. "Those kids," he said. "They got no respect for nothing." To Engel he said, "You drive again."

Fox said, "Are you crazy?"

"Engel won't try nothing. Will you, Engel?"

Engel would, but he said, "Not me. I know you guys."

"That's right," said Gittel. "He'll play on our sympathy, and on friendship, and he'll try to buy us off, but he won't pull anything cute, will you, Engel?"

"You know me, I guess," said Engel.

Fox said, "I am doubtful. I just want you to know that."

They all got into the car again, Engel behind the wheel and the other two in back. Fox let Engel know he had his gun out and ready for anything, and Gittel again told Fox there was nothing to worry about. Engel asked where to now and Gittel said, "Triborough Bridge. Up to a Hundred Twenny-fifth Street."

"Right."

Engel bided his time. He concentrated a lot of his attention on the car, shifting constantly back and forth, pushing the car uptown practically by physical strength. He also, in order to keep Gittel and Fox unsuspicious, talked away to the two in the back seat, using the exact techniques Gittel had prescribed for him, alluding to their past friendship, trying for their sympathy, subtly leaving himself open to suggestion on bribes. But he didn't expect any of this to do him any immediate good. What he had to do, somewhere along the line, was purely and simply get away from these two.

The tollbooths for the Triborough Bridge were right up in the middle of the bridge. Engel contemplated simply getting out of the car there and walking away, doubting that Gittel and Fox would dare shoot him next to the tollbooths, but the problem was there was nowhere to run away *to*. If the tollbooths had been down at ground level he might have tried it, but not this way, stuck on the bridge on foot.

After the bridge they directed him onto the Grand Central Parkway, which curved around through Queens. "Take it to the Long Island Expressway," Gittel told him, "then take the Expressway east." Which meant out on the Island, out away from New York.

Grand Central Parkway was landscaped on both sides, with a central mall. Now, a little after one o'clock in the morning, there wasn't much traffic moving in either direction.

Engel waited, biding his time. He stayed in the farthest left lane of the three, driving at about forty miles an hour.

He waited, driving along, talking to the two guys in the back seat, and finally the conditions were just right. There was no traffic near him in any lane. The road was straight. There were no overpasses immediately ahead.

He put the gear shift in neutral, opened the door, and rolled out onto the mall. As he left, he heard somebody say, "Hey!"

It was quite a sensation, hitting turf at forty miles an hour. Engel had rolled himself into a ball as he was leaving the car, and now he just went tumbling forward, end over end, until he gradually lost momentum and opened out flat on his back in the middle of the greenery.

He sat up, with difficulty, finding himself dizzy and a little nauseous. Ahead of him and still pulling away, down now to about twenty miles an hour but far from stopped, the black Chevy was still moving along. It had drifted over to the center lane, but was still going pretty straight. Kenny would see to things like wheel balancing and front-end alignment.

Engel could imagine Gittel and Fox in the back seat, both scrabbling to get up front, to climb over the seat, each getting in the other's way, the both of them shouting and jumping and wasting energy.

While Engel wasted time.

Right. He got to his feet—he seemed to have muscle aches in about thirty different places—staggered over the mall, across the eastbound lanes of traffic, over the turf on the other side to the metal fence there, climbed the fence, attained one of the little dim streets of Queens, and ran for his life.

17

IN THE MANHATTAN PHONE book there were six columns of people named Rose. In the Queens phone book there were three and a half columns of people named Rose. And the particular Rose that Engel was looking for could just as easily live in Brooklyn or The Bronx. Or Long Island. Or Westchester. Or Staten Island. Or New Jersey. Or Connecticut. Or on the Moon.

Engel shut the two directories and went back to his table, where his coffee was cooling and his cheese Danish was aging. He sat down, glumly took a mouthful of Danish, and looked out the window while he chewed.

He was in an all-night diner on 31st Street in Queens, about half a mile from Grand Central Parkway. He'd run this far full tilt, and here for the moment he'd gone to ground, and he'd been here fifteen minutes now without yet being able to think what he should do next.

Very little was clear to him, but included with that little was the indisputable fact he'd been framed. He'd been framed neatly, sweetly and completely, and not only that but he'd been framed by a stranger. In fact, if he'd heard the conversation right, it was a whole group of strangers. The little guy named Rose had only been representing others like himself.

Would Nick Rovito have taken the unsubstantiated word of a schmo like Rose? No. Nick Rovito would have insisted on the names of other businessmen who would tell the same story, and then he would have checked with those businessmen. That they had told the same story was pretty clear.

In other words, a whole group of complete strangers had taken it into their heads to frame a guy named Engel. Now, why would a whole group of complete strangers want to do a thing like that?

Businessmen, too. Solid citizens. Not maniacs, not practical jokers, not a rival mob, nothing like that at all. Husbands and fathers, proprietors of business establishments, payers of taxes, these were the men who had suddenly and inexplicably exerted themselves to put the finger on a guy they didn't even know.

Why?

Slurping at cold coffee, watching the dark empty street outside the diner window, Engel gnawed at that question and his cheese Danish in equal portions, and whereas he was gradually getting somewhere with the Danish he was getting nowhere at all with the question.

With the Danish gone, with nothing but dregs left in the coffee cup, he decided it was best to table the question awhile and devote himself to thinking about another and a more immediate problem.

Like, where now?

He couldn't go back to the apartment, that was obvious. If Nick Rovito's boys weren't there by now, the cops would be. (It was hard to keep in mind, but that was an additional complication: the cops either already were or soon would be after him for the murder of Willy Menchik. As if he didn't have enough trouble without!) So the apartment was forbidden territory. So was his mother's place. So, in fact, was any place he'd ever been before.

He thought fleetingly of Dolly, who even now he could surely reach through her friend Roxanne. But the way Dolly was leaving notes around, one of them was bound to be picked up by *somebody* dangerous, which meant that Dolly, too, soon or late, would be watched.

Money? He had about forty bucks on him, less than he usually carried but he'd insisted on paying for dinner up in Connecticut tonight. He also had a watch he could probably pawn in the morning.

In a second of real despair, he thought of turning himself in to the cops. In exchange for protection and leniency, he could promise to sing for them, do them a Valachi. Of course, there wouldn't be a chance he'd ever convince them he'd been framed on the Menchik murder, which meant he'd spend the rest of his life—long or short, but probably short—behind bars, and that was almost as bad as not having any life to spend at all.

No. There had to be another way, a better way.

In order, then; take everything in order. The first thing to do was find a safe place to hole up for a while. The second thing to do was find out or figure out why he'd been framed, and the third thing to do was somehow prove to Nick Rovito that it was a frame.

"You want anything else?"

It was the waitress, a woman as stocky as she was surly, who looked in her white uniform like a sadistic nurse. Engel looked at her and shook his head. "Just the check."

She slapped it down on the table as though she were trumping his ace, and waddled away again in triumph. Engel left a nickel tip, paid the man behind the counter, and left the diner.

Outside, on the corner, there was a cabstand, with one lone taxi sitting there all forlorn, its vacancy light glumly burning on its roof, its driver slouched behind the wheel with a copy of the *Daily News* up in front of his face. He also wore a cap, and had a pencil behind his ear. He also chewed gum.

Engel stood irresolutely on the sidewalk. If he could think of somewhere to go, he'd use this cab to get there. But first he had to think of a place, a place he could get to but where no one would think of looking for him. Either with someone he knew, or maybe even a place that was deserted, where there—

Got it.

Engel snapped his fingers, and allowed a faint ray of hope to soar up his spinal column and light up, briefly, his gloomy mind. Part one worked out; nothing left now but parts two and three.

He went over to the cab, slid into the back seat, and said, "Manhattan. West 71st Street."

The driver slowly turned his head, and said, "Manhattan? Why don't you take the subway, Mac? Cabs cost too much."

"I'm in a hurry," Engel told him.

"I don't like Manhattan," the driver said. "You want to go some place in Queens, any place in Queens, just let me know."

"You can't turn down a fare," Engel said. "It's against the law."

"You gonna be a hardnose? Give me an address in Queens, I'll take you."

"Good. The nearest precinct house."

The driver squeezed his face up. "What, to turn me in?"

"You know it."

The driver sighed, and folded up his paper, and faced front. "I hate hardnoses," he said.

Engel lit a cigarette and blew smoke at the back of the driver's neck. "Tough," he said, because that's the way he felt.

Once he got moving, the driver was one of the fastest men afloat. He was clearly in a hurry to deliver Engel to Manhattan, turn around, and get the hell back to his beloved Queens.

They tore down 31st Street to Northern Boulevard, to the Queensboro Bridge approach, over the bridge, up Third Avenue to 66th Street, west across 66th Street through Central Park and over to Broadway, up Broadway to West 71st Street, and over 71st Street to the address Engel wanted, which was a good block from where he intended to go.

The meter read a dollar eighty-five. Engel gave him two dollars and waited for his change. The driver gave it to him, frowning, watching as though he didn't believe it, and Engel pocketed the fifteen cents, got out of the cab, and slammed the door. The driver said several things, several very angry things, but he was already racing down the block as he said them, so Engel didn't hear the exact words. Still, he caught the drift.

He went up the steps of the nearest building, and when the cab turned the far corner he came back down them again and walked the block to where he wanted to go. The downstairs door was open, and he hurried up the stairs without seeing anyone, stopping in front of the door behind which Charlie Brody had lived his life.

It was the perfect spot. Brody's wife wouldn't be coming here for at least a few days more, nor would anyone else be dropping by. Engel and Brody hadn't been close friends while Brody was alive, so there was no reason for anyone to think of Engel in relation to Brody's apartment now. Here, in safety and comfort, he could proceed to parts two and three, the why of his framing and the process of getting himself unframed.

The apartment door, of course, was locked, but Engel was in no mood to let that stop him. Judging by the other doors on this floor, and remembering what the inside of the apartment had looked like, he figured out just where and how much of the area of this floor belonged to the Brody apartment, and then he turned away and went on up the rest of the stairs to the roof.

The night was still beautiful, as beautiful as on the ride to Connecticut, but Engel was no longer of a disposition to notice it. He crossed the roof to the rear wall, where the top rungs of a fire escape curved up into sight, and looked over the edge. At each level there was a broad platform, stretching across in front of two windows, one each for adjoining apartments. Two floors down, the window on the right belonged, so far as Engel could judge, to the Brody apartment. To the bedroom, in fact.

Creeping carefully down the fire escape, Engel reflected bitterly that he seemed to be branching out into all sorts of new crimes lately: grave robbing, truck stealing, now breaking and entering. Walking on Grand Central Parkway, there was another offense. Leaving an automobile at forty miles an hour was probably against the law too, and earlier today he'd come perilously close to impersonating a policeman.

"Great," he muttered. "I'm becoming the Renaissance man of the underworld."

The window, when he reached it, was locked, just as the door had been. But Engel would waste no time with windows. The upper half of this one was divided into six small panes; taking off his shoe, Engel used the heel to smash in the middle pane in the lower row, the one by the lock. The noise this made was loud, but brief, and Engel doubted anyone would pay attention to it. New Yorkers needed a noise that lasted half an hour or so before they'd begin to wonder if something was up, and even then most of them would avoid going to see what it was.

Engel reached in past the jagged edges of glass, undid the window catch, and then pushed the lower half of the window up and climbed through. He shut the window behind him again, pulled the shade all the way down, and then felt his way around the room, hitting his shin against various anonymous but hard objects, until he found the doorway on the opposite side, beside which was the switch for the light. Engel pushed it, the overhead light came on, and Bobbi Bounds Brody sat up in the bed, saying, "Mr. Engel, you scared the life out of me."

Engel blinked at her. "I thought," he said, "I thought you moved out."

"It felt so funny, sleeping somewheres else. I know I got to move in with Marge and Tinkerbell eventually, but for now I'd rather stay right here, with my memories. Coming back with you like I did this evening, remembering all the good times and like that, I knew, I just knew I wasn't ready yet to move out. So here I am."

Engel nodded. "Here you are all right," he said.

"Mr. Engel, why didn't you knock on the door?"

"I didn't think anybody was home."

"I would of given you a key. All you had to do was call Archie Freihofer, he'd have fixed it up so you could get the key."

"It's kind of complicated, Mrs. Brody."

She shook her head. "You shouldn't call me Mrs. Brody," she said. "That isn't my name any more, and I got to get used to it. You better call me Bobbi."

Engel looked at her. She was holding the pale green blanket up to her neck as she sat there in bed, and above it her friendly but not particularly bright face gazed earnestly and sincerely at him. "Okay, Bobbi," he said. "I need somebody to talk to, somebody I can trust. I want to make it you."

"Well, gee, Mr. Engel." Her eyes widened with a combination of surprise and pleasure and curiosity. "You sit down here," she said, one bare arm emerging from around the pale green blanket to pat the bed. "You sit right down here and tell me all about it."

Engel sat down, near the foot of the bed. "To make it short and sweet," he said, "I been framed. It's a double frame, both with Nick Rovito and with the cops."

"Holy cow," she said.

"You bet. Nick Rovito himself set up the frame with the cops, to keep things neat and simple after a couple of the boys should rub me out."

"Rub you out? Mr. Engel, you don't mean it."

"Yes, I do. He must of called the Committee last night and got their okay. I suppose that's why he had to set up the other frame."

"What?"

Engel suddenly realized he'd gradually stopped talking to her and started talking to himself. He shook his head and said, "Let me try and say it straight. Some people framed me with Nick Rovito, told him I was doing something I wasn't doing. So Nick planned to bump me off, and on the side set up a frame with the cops, so they wouldn't look too hard for who killed me."

Eyes wide, mouth open, she nodded her head slowly. "I *think* I got it," she said.

"I feel the same way you do," Engel told her. "I can't figure it out."

She said, "Who was it framed you with Mr. Rovito?"

"That's just it," Engel said. "That's just the part that's crazy. It was businessmen, legit straight honest businessmen. Not guys in the organization at all. And not only that, but businessmen I don't even know, businessmen I never even met before."

"Well, maybe it's a mistake, then."

Engel shook his head. "One of them identified me. 'That's him,' he said to Nick. I was right there."

"Boy," she said. "That's terrible."

"And I can't figure it out. Why should they do it to me?"

She said, "Well, maybe to stop you from doing whatever you were doing."

He frowned at her. "What? I told you already, it was a frame, I *wasn't* doing what they said I was doing."

"No, no, that isn't what I mean. I mean what you were *really* doing. Maybe they wanted to stop you from doing what you *were* doing. Maybe you were on a job or something that was going to hurt them later on."

Engel stared at her. "You just thought that up?" he said. "All by yourself?"

"Well, I only thought—"

"No, I'm not putting you down. What I mean is, I never even thought of it that way."

She blinked, a couple of times. "You think maybe that's it?"

"Why not? It's anyway a reason, right? That's what was driving me nuts all this time, I couldn't even think of a reason. Right or wrong, that doesn't matter yet, just so I have some kind of reason why that guy Rose fingered me, so I can at least start thinking about it."

She said, "What was that name?"

Hope sprang again within Engel's breast. "Rose," he said, and waited.

But all she said was, "That's a girl's name."

Engel sagged a little. "It's his last name," he said.

"Oh. Well, anyway, if you could figure out what you were doing that they didn't want you to do, maybe you could figure out why they did this thing."

"Yeah," said Engel. "Yeah, that's the rub." He got to his feet, and lit a cigarette, and started pacing back and forth at the foot of the bed. "That's the rub," he said again.

What had he been doing? Looking for Charlie Brody, that's all. Was there anything else, anything he'd been in the middle of before the Charlie Brody thing came up? No. Anything for the near future, that he was supposed to get to as soon as the Charlie Brody thing was done? No.

Charlie Brody? They didn't want him to find Charlie Brody? What kind of sense did that make, a bunch of legitimate businessmen didn't want him to find a dead body? No sense at all, that's what kind.

Bobbi finally broke the silence, saying, "Would it help you to talk some more? Is what you were doing anything you could talk about?"

He looked at her. Up to now he'd been keeping the essential fact away from her in order to protect her feelings, but the way she had of all of a sudden seeing answers, maybe he ought to spill everything to her. Besides, if she knew about the swiping of her husband, she might be able to throw some light on it, might be able to think of something in Brody's past that would tell them where he might be found now.

He sat down on the bed again. "Bobbi," he said. "I got something to tell you, and maybe you ought to brace yourself."

"Brace myself?"

"It's about Charlie."

"Brace myself? About Charlie? Charlie's *dead,* Mr. Engel, what's there left to brace myself about?"

"Yeah, well, just wait. Do you know very much about what Charlie's job was?"

"Well, sure. Husband and wife don't have secrets, why should they? He used to carry stuff, down South and back." She made a shooting gesture with her visible hand at the arm still hidden by the blanket. "Snow," she said.

"Do you know how?" Engel asked her. "How he carried the stuff and didn't get caught?"

She shrugged like an Italian. "I dunno. In a suitcase, I guess. He never said nothing."

"In a suit," Engel told her.

She wrinkled up her cheeks and nose. "Huh?"

"In the blue suit. Sewed in the lining. Bobbi, he was buried with a quarter million bucks' worth of snow in that blue suit."

"Holy Peoria! You mean it?"

"I mean it."

She shook her head. "Boy! I'm surprised they don't send somebody out to dig him up and get the suit back. Boy."

"They did," Engel told her. "Me. I dug him up."

"You did? How was he?"

"Gone."

"What's that?"

"We didn't bury him, Bobbi. That's what you got to brace yourself for. We buried an empty casket. Somebody swiped Charlie."

"A Dr. Frankenstein!" she shouted, eyes widening, both hands coming up to be pressed palm-in against her cheeks. The blanket fell away.

Engel politely turned his head, because it was obvious she didn't wear anything to bed but a ribbon in her hair. "No," he said to the opposite wall, "it wouldn't be anything like that, not in the twentieth century."

"Oh, my gosh. You can turn again, Mr. Engel, it's okay now."

He turned, and she had the blanket back up where it belonged. "That's what I been doing," he said, "is looking for Charlie."

"I want to thank you for looking the other way, Mr. Engel," she said. "When a gentleman treats a lady like a lady, it makes her feel especially like a lady, if you know what I mean."

"Oh, sure. Any time."

"And you been looking for Charlie? That's awful nice, Mr. Engel."

"Well, it was my job. Nick wanted that suit awful bad."

"Boy, I guess so." She cocked her head to one side. "Why'd anybody want to swipe Charlie?" she said. "That's an awful thing to do, that's disrespectful of the dead, to swipe their bodies."

"And that's all I been doing," Engel said. "So if that guy Rose and his other businessmen were trying to stop me from doing what I was doing, it was looking for Charlie that I was doing. You wouldn't know anybody named Rose, would you?"

"A colored lady, used to clean the apartment. No men."

"This guy runs a business of some kind. Maybe a store or some kind of factory or something."

She shook her head, back and forth. "I'm sorry, Mr. Engel, but if I'd ever met any man named Rose, front name *or* last name, I'd remember it."

Engel spread his hands helplessly, and got up again from the bed. "That's it," he said. "That's where I am right now. I got away from the guys that were supposed to take care of me, and I figured I could hide out here overnight because there wouldn't be anybody here and nobody'd think to look here for me."

"Well, you can stay," she said. "You know that, Mr. Engel."

"If anybody finds out I was here, they could make it rough on you. Either the organization or the cops, both."

"Oh, foo," she said, and waved it all away with her visible hand. "Nobody ever bothers about me. Besides, who's going to tell them you were here? You won't, and I won't, and that's all of us there is."

"I'll clear out first thing in the morning," Engel told her. "What I got to do, I got to keep looking for Charlie. If I can find out where Charlie is, maybe that'll explain everything else."

"Mr. Engel, I'll be eternally grateful to you for looking for Charlie. I can't tell you how much I appreciate it."

"Well, I'll do my best," Engel told her, "for both Charlie's sake and my own." He looked around, said, "We can talk some more in the morning, if you want. I'll go sleep on the sofa in the living room."

She shook her head, solemnly. "No, you won't," she said.

"What?"

She said, "There isn't much I can do to help you find Charlie, or help you get out of this jam you're in. There aren't too many ways I can express my appreciation, but there is one. You turn the light out and come on over here."

Engel made a vague sort of gesture. "Uhh," he said, "I oughta just—"

"This is just between us," she said. "Just friends, no charge or anything like that."

Engel cleared his throat, and said, "Now, you don't have to feel obligated or any—"

"I don't feel obligated," she said. "I feel that we're friends, and friends ought to do for each other, and there isn't much I can do for you but what I can I will. And be more than happy."

Engel was going to go on protesting, but then he took a closer look at her face, and he could see in her eyes that if he didn't accept her invitation her feelings would be hurt very badly. Very badly.

Well. One thing about Engel, he always was gallant.

18

HE WAS SNOW WHITE, in a glass coffin, and the Seven Dwarfs were burying him alive. He didn't seem to be able to move. He hollered at them, but they couldn't hear him through the glass, and they just carried him over to the hole and put him down in it and started shoveling dirt in. One of them looked like Nick Rovito, and one of them looked like Augustus Merriweather, and one of them looked like Deputy Inspector Callaghan. Two others looked like Gittel and Fox, another one looked like Kurt Brock, and the last one looked like Bashful.

Bashful threw a golden rose in on the casket, and the others all started shoveling dirt. Dirt was bouncing on the glass top of the casket, making him blink because it kept looking as though the dirt was going to come right down on his face. But the glass was in the way, and the dirt landed on it with thud sounds. Thud, thud, thud. And for every thud, he blinked.

It was the blinking woke him up. One of the blinks was so real that he actually opened his eyes on the other side of it, and there were no Seven Dwarfs, there was no glass casket, there was no dirt, no rose, no grave. There was a ceiling with cracks in it, and there was a strange bedroom with muted golden light coming through a window with the shade pulled all the way down.

He blinked once more, while shifting from the dream world to whatever sort of world this was, and then memory and reality and a sense of place came back, and he sat up, looking all over the bed for Bobbi.

She wasn't there, but on the night table there was a note. Engel reached over, picked it up, and read:

Dear Mister Engel,

Archie Freihofer wanted me to start back to work today so I am supposed to go over to the Coliseum, there is some sort of Home Furnishings Fair going on there and they will want some girls for the buyers and the "visiting firemen" but why they always want to interview the girls in the morning I do not know but that is the way they are.

I will probably not be back tonight so if you want to sleep here again you had better come in the window once more which I will leave unlocked.

There is instant coffee and English muffins and anything else in the kitchen for breakfast.

Good luck and I know Charlie would thank you for your efforts on his behalf just as much as I do.

Sincerely yours,
Bobbi Bounds

PS. If your underwear and socks are not dry

take some from the middle drawer of the
dresser, it is all right. BB

"Underwear and socks?" Engel looked up from the note,
and took quick stock. On the chair by the desk his shirt was
neatly hung, his tie draped over it. On the hook on the inside
of the open closet door was his suit, neatly placed on a hang-
er. When he leaned to the left he could see his shoes on the
floor beside the bed. But his underwear and socks?

Still a bit befuddled by the Seven Dwarfs, but also confused by the note and in a half-awake panic about his underwear and socks, Engel staggered out of the bed and went padding naked from the room in search of his missing garments.

They were in the bathroom, on wire hangers hung on the
shower curtain bar over the tub. And they were still wet, or
at least damp. "Well," he muttered. "Fine." He went padding
back to the bedroom.

As he put on a pair of Charlie Brody's shorts, the thought
came to him that he was getting far too closely enmeshed
with Charlie Brody, that his own life was being bound up
to an unhealthy degree with the past and present of Charlie Brody. "Just let me get you planted where you belong," he
muttered. "That's all, just let me get this mess straightened
out. Then you and me are quits, Charlie."

An hour later, washed and dressed and breakfasted, he
felt much better. He'd slept late and it was now nearly noon;
time to be doing.

Doing what? With Bobbi's help he'd figured a couple of
things out last night, but he was still almost completely in
the dark. He didn't know who to blame for anything, didn't
know who to ask questions of nor even what questions to ask,

and even if he did know any, his mobility was severely limited at the moment by the fact that both the cops and the organization would be scouring the city for him by now.

Sitting there over a third cup of instant coffee and his second cigarette, he thought about what to do next. If only, he thought, if only there was someone he could send out to do the legwork for him while he himself remained safely out of sight. Get somebody maybe that the organization didn't even know, like Dolly for instance or—

Somebody they didn't know.

Like he didn't know Rose. Like that

He squinted in a cloud of cigarette smoke and worked that one out. He didn't know Rose. Rose had framed him to stop him from doing what he was doing, which was looking for Charlie Brody. Rose had done it on behalf of somebody else, somebody Engel *did* know.

"Oh ho," he said. Out loud. "Somebody I know doesn't want me looking for Charlie Brody. This somebody has a way to put pressure on this guy Rose and some other businessmen to make them say stuff to frame me."

All well and good, but what did it mean?

"It means," Engel said aloud, "it means I was getting close. I didn't know it myself, but somewhere along the line I started to get close, and I made this somebody nervous enough to fix me."

Right. Engel dropped his cigarette in his coffee, got up from the table, and went back to the bedroom, where he sat at the little desk and armed himself with pencil and paper. The thing to do now was make a list of every single person he'd talked to since he'd started looking for Charlie Brody. Thinking back, he gradually compiled his list:

>Mrs. Brody
>Margo Kane
>Inspector Callaghan
>Kurt Brock
>Fred Harwell
>Archie Freihofer

Some list. Squinting at it, tapping it now and again with his pencil, Engel kept trying to find somebody on it who might have a hankering to steal Charlie Brody, to frame Engel, to murder Merriweather, but nobody seemed at all right for the job.

Mrs. Brody? Bobbi? What would she swipe her husband for? How would she be able to pressure Rose into helping with the frame? Well, she might have met Rose while she was working for Archie Freihofer before she got married, and she might be able to blackmail him, threaten to go to his wife or something. She *could,* maybe, but there was no sense in it. No, and she was too open, too guileless; she'd never be able to run a scheme as complicated as this one was getting.

Margo Kane? In the first place she already had a dead husband, so what would she need with somebody else's? In the second place there wasn't any connection that Engel had found between Margo Kane and Charlie Brody in Brody's lifetime, so why should there be any connection now? As a matter of fact, Margo didn't even know Engel was looking for Brody's body, so she couldn't very well be the one trying to stop him from finding it.

Callaghan? As with everybody else, there was no reason for him to want a body. Beyond that, Callaghan was just too damn honest, honest to the point of stubborn bullheadedness, far too honest to be involved in anything as shady as all this. He might have been able to pressure Rose, but other than that he was out of it. He was involved, as was Margo Kane, merely through the circumstance of having been at the grief parlor the same time as Engel.

Kurt Brock? He'd admitted he was the next to the last person to see Charlie Brody's corpse, but other than that he seemed to have no connection with anything. None with Brody, none with Rose. No motive for anything. In fact, he was the only one in the crowd who couldn't possibly be the guy Engel was after, if he assumed the guy he wanted was also the killer of Merri-weather. Brock was covered on that, and if Callaghan had accepted his alibi it was good enough for Engel.

Fred Harwell? He was almost the only one who'd known about the value of the suit, but Fred would surely have been content to swipe the suit instead of the whole body. Unless, of course, there'd been a time factor, and it was simpler to just take the whole body and go rather than stick around trying to get the suit off it. But Harwell had been in the organization for years, and knew the score; he wouldn't be dumb enough to try something cute like this. As to setting up Rose, Harwell was a possible but hardly a probable.

Archie Freihofer? All Archie knew or cared about was his women. It was impossible to see Archie stealing dead bodies, particularly male bodies, impossible to see him stabbing Merri-weather or scheming with Rose or any of the rest of it.

Yeah, but that was the trouble. It was impossible to see *any* of these people doing any of the things that some one of them sure as hell had done.

Unless, of course, there was a name missing from this list, somebody Engel hadn't gotten onto yet.

But if Engel hadn't come across him yet, the bastard, why should he sic Rose on Engel?

He shook his head and went over the whole thing again, and over it again, and over it again. Of the six people on the list, he could think of only one with even a hint of a motive for stealing Charlie Brody, and that was Fred Harwell. He'd been Brody's boss, he'd known what was in the suit. But of course Fred swore he hadn't known until too late that the suit had been used to bury Brody in. But still . . .

Fred Harwell? He *might* have taken the body, if the suit was too tough to get off in a hurry. He *might* have set up Rose, it was possible Fred had the contacts for a piece of work like that. And he *might* have killed Merriweather, if he and Merriweather had been in on the body snatching together or if Fred was afraid Merriweather had found out the truth somehow and might talk.

It all seemed so unlikely. Yet it was the only possibility Engel seemed able to come up with, so finally he decided there was nothing to do but follow it up. He'd go back and see each of the people on this list a second time, no matter how unlikely they seemed, and this time he'd see could he find the links in the chain. And he'd start off with Fred Harwell.

He left a note for Bobbi:

> Thanks for the hospitality. I had a good sleep
> and a good breakfast. I'll be in touch, if I get
> the chance.

He didn't sign it, just in case the wrong eyes saw it; he didn't want to get her in trouble. He left it propped on the kitchen table and went out of the apartment.

Down on the street there was a red and yellow truck with a carnival-type ride on the back, gaily painted little spaceships that went around and around a central hub where the motor was mounted, while a loudspeaker on the roof of the truck cab blared rock and roll from a radio station. Grinning children whirled around while more children stood in line beside the truck, waiting their turn.

Engel stopped and looked at it, feeling nostalgia for the simple days of his own childhood in Washington Heights. These trucks plied the poorer neighborhoods of New York all spring and summer, one of the city's less odious harbingers of the warm months. This was the first one Engel had seen this year, and it affected him much the way the first robin affects the country dweller.

Until, that is, the loudspeaker finished its rock and roll and segued into the news. The children in their tin spaceships now whirled around to the tensions of the day, which included:

"Police today are searching for Aloysius Eugene Engel, alleged gangland killer, who last night shot and killed in Jersey City—"

And so on. With description: "Engel is described as six foot one inch tall, sallow complexion, dark brown hair and brown eyes, strong build. He is believed to be armed and dangerous."

Unarmed, feeling anything but dangerous, Engel fled away down the sidewalk.

He was a block and a half away before he remembered his underwear was still in Bobbi's bathroom.

19

TO LOOK AT FRED Harwell's place of business, you'd never know he had charge of a multimillion-dollar operation with employees in the hundreds and customers in the tens of thousands. But, on the other hand, Fred Harwell's operation was not the sort of business that put up glass buildings to itself on Fifth Avenue. Given the nature of his trade, a grimy and bankrupt-looking brick building on Tenth Avenue was just the perfect location for his home office.

This building was between 45th and 46th streets. The first and second floors housed a Spanish-language phonograph record company that specialized in low-fi records of people shaking gourds. The fourth floor was the office and warehouse of a company that sold odd-looking women's underwear via mail order and did all its advertising in muscleman magazines. Between these two, on the third floor, behind the name Afro-Indic Importing Corporation, lurked Fred Harwell and his organization of dope peddlers.

Another of those carnival-ride trucks was parked just down the block from this building as Engel arrived, but was happily playing music instead of Engel's description. Engel walked past it, went into Fred's building, and up the two flights of murky grimy stairs to the third floor, where there was a short hallway and two doors, one unmarked and one lettered AFRO-INDIC IMPORTING CORP.

The main motif up here was ancient wood flooring, with broad dust-filled holes between the slats. Cracked and dented plaster walls were painted a heavy shade of green reminiscent of the interior of the Minotaur's stomach, and from somewhere there came a pervasive odor of soggy moldering cardboard.

Engel pushed open the door and entered a small barren room containing a wooden desk, a wooden filing cabinet, a hat rack, two huge dusty windows bare of curtains or blinds or drapes, a crumbling brown leather sofa, and Fred Harwell's mistress name of Fancy, who was very plain.

Engel had no idea if Fancy knew the latest on himself, so he just bluffed it through to see what would happen. "Hi, Fancy," he said. "I come to see Fred."

She looked surprised, but that was only natural; he didn't come around here very often. "He's in," she said. "You want I should announce you?"

"Naw, that's okay." Engel waved airily and crossed the room and pushed open the other door on its far side.

Fred Harwell looked up from his desk, where he'd been hard at work on last Sunday's *Times* crossword puzzle. "All" he said, and then, as realization struck him, "Al? For Christ's sake, Al—"

Engel shut the door. "Not a word, Fred," he said. "Play it very cool."

"Al, what are you doing here? Do you know how hot you are?"

"Yeah, I know how hot I am. What I don't know is who lit the fire under me."

Fred pressed the palms of his hands against his chest. "All *Me?*"

"You tell me."

"Why would I, Al? Answer me that, why would I?"

"I don't know yet. I got theories, that's all."

Fred shook his head back and forth. "This is crazy," he said. "Everything's crazy. One second I'm sitting here doing my job like always, everything's jake, and the next second you come in and say I did something to you. Like what? Like how? Like why?"

Engel said, "What about me? One second I'm doing my job like always and the next second I'm a dead man, I got the cops and the organization *both* after me."

Fred raised both hands, palms up. "Al, that's the chance you took," he said. "I always figured you were too smart to try a stunt like that, but there you are. And if it got back to Nick Rovito, why figure I or anybody else did it to you? You did it to yourself, Al."

"Now wait a second," said Engel. "Hold on a second, there. That was a frame-up, Fred. I never been on the take in my life."

"Then I'm sorry. If that's true, I'm sorry, Al, but what can *I* do? I can't talk to Nick, I can't—"

Engel decided to throw a curve and see what happened. "I just been to see Rose," he said.

Fred squinted. "Rose who?"

"You don't know who Rose is?"

"One of Archie's girls?"

"Come off it, Fred. Rose is a man and you know it."

Fred blinked several times, then suddenly flashed a very weak and shaky smile. "Oh, yeah," he said. He was leaning farther back in his chair now, farther away from Engel. "Yeah, that's right," he said. "Rose is a man, I forgot that."

"What are you doing, you simple bastard? Are you *humoring* me?"

"Oh, no," said Fred. "No, no, Al, not a bit of it."

"Rose is a *last* name, too, you moron. Like Billy Rose. You gonna tell me *Billy* Rose is a woman?"

Fred had to wait a few seconds to shift gears all over again, and then he said, "Oh. I see what you mean. A *guy* named Rose, that's his last name it isn't his first name. Al, I didn't know, with everything so crazy all of a sudden I didn't know but what maybe you, too, you know, maybe the strain of overwork or something, you can't be sure about things like that . . ." and trailed away.

Engel said, "Shut up, Fred."

"Yes," said Fred. "Right."

Engel paced back and forth, back and forth, frowning with concentration. Fred was in the clear, that was obvious. He was the only one Engel had had even a glimmer on for motive and opportunity, and the bastard was clean. It just wasn't possible that Fred was lying, that Fred was the one behind all this.

Fred, after a couple of minutes, said, "Can I say something, Al?"

"Speak."

"As soon as you leave here, I got to call Nick and tell him you were here. You understand that."

Engel nodded. "Yeah, I understand that."

"I got a wife and kids, Al. I got Fancy. I got responsibilities, and that means I got to cover myself."

"Yeah yeah yeah."

"Al, I want you to know, for what it's worth, I believe you. I known you a number of years now, and while we never been real close friends we always got along together and I always considered you a good reliable type and a pleasant personality. So if you tell me it's a frame, I take your word for it. That don't cut no ice with Nick, that don't change anything at all in fact, but I want you to know."

"Yeah. Thanks, Fred."

"I wish I could help."

"Yeah. You can, Fred."

Fred had been looking very sincere. Now his expression changed, and he began to look like a man who, in the middle of a speech to a crowd of five thousand, has begun to suspect his fly is open. He said, "I can?"

"You can find out for me about Rose."

"Rose."

"I want to know Rose's first name, and I want to know where I can find him."

"I thought you already talked to him."

"No. Don't worry about that. I know he's a businessman, this Rose, on the legit somewhere but connected with the organization. There had to be somebody he could talk to when he started to put the finger on me. It's a safe bet he didn't go to Nick direct."

Fred said, "Then who?"

Engel said, "Rapaport."

"Rapaport? Why Rapaport?"

"Because Rapaport is our union man. Rapaport controls the union end of the organization just the way you control the dope end and Archie controls the girl end. And the quickest connection a businessman will have with the organization is through a union."

Fred said, "Granted. That's okay, that's smart, but then what? You should go see Rapaport, not me."

"I can't wander all over town, Fred. Remember? I'm hot."

Fred said, "What can I do?"

"You can call Rapaport."

"What? Are you out of your skull, Al?"

"No. You can call Rapaport and you can ask him about Rose."

"Why? How? What's my excuse?"

Engel shook his head, thinking hard. "You say to him, uh, you say, 'Listen, there used to be a guy name of Rose owned this building, we had some trouble with him, I wonder is he the same one Engel was holding up?' Then Rapaport tells you about Rose."

"What if he don't?"

Engel said, "Then you tried, that's all. You tried."

"Al, I honest to God don't want to do it."

Engel put his right hand palm up on the middle of Fred's desk. He had a large hand with big knuckles. He said, "You see that hand, Fred?"

Fred said, "Yeah, I see it."

"For purposes of discussion," Engel said, "let's us call that hand a lethal weapon."

"Yeah?"

"Then let's say you can tell Nick you had to make the call because I threatened you with a lethal weapon."

"But—"

"And just so you won't have to lie," Engel said, closing the hand into a fist, "I *will* threaten you with it." He raised the fist off the desk and held it close to Fred's face.

Fred looked at it, sort of cross-eyed. He said, "But what if Nick don't believe me?"

"I tell you what I'll do," Engel said. "If you don't think you can put the story over, I'll hit you once or twice, give you a couple marks. Not because I'm mad or anything like that, but just to help you convince Nick. Okay by you?"

"Wait a second, Al, uh, wait a second."

"It's up to you, Fred."

Fred looked at the fist, and licked his lips, and tried various expressions for his face, and finally cleared his throat and nodded and said, "Okay."

"Okay? Okay what?"

"Okay I'll make the call. And you don't have to leave marks, it's okay. You don't have to do a thing."

"I just want to be helpful," Engel told him. "That's the way we all ought to be, helpful to one another."

"I said I'd do it."

Engel straightened and spread his hands. "And I thank you, Fred," he said.

Fred made the call, and while he talked Engel leaned down close beside his ear so he could hear both ends of the conversation. It went:

Fred: Hi, this is Fred.

Rapaport: Hi, Fred, whadaya say?

Fred: That was really something about Engel, huh?

Rapaport: You never know what goes on inside a guy's head, I've said it time and time again.

Fred: You know, that guy Engel was holding up, that Rose, he—

Rapaport: Rose? How'd you hear about him?

Fred: Oh, uh . . . (Engel whispered, "From Nick.") . . . From Nick.

Rapaport: Yeah? That's funny. He said he wanted that kept quiet.

Fred: Yeah, he told me the same thing. About this guy Rose, there was a guy name of Rose used to own this building, you know where I am on Tenth Avenue?

Rapaport: Is that right?

Fred: Yeah. We had trouble with this Rose, I remember, he was very down on the organization. I wonder could it be the same guy. What's your Rose's name?

Rapaport: Herbert. Herbert Rose.

Fred: Oh. No, this guy was Louie Rose.

Rapaport: It's a pretty common name, Rose.

Fred: I guess so. This Herbert, he's in real estate?

Rapaport: Naw, trucking. He's got a nickel-dime delivery outfit over by the piers on the West Side.

Fred: Oh. Then there's no connection, I guess.

Rapaport: With your Rose? It don't look like it.

Fred: I just thought, if it was the same Rose, there might be more to it than Nick knew about.

Rapaport: You don't think Engel did it?

Fred: Well, you never know, isn't that right?

Rapaport: Well, don't say nothing like that to Nick. He's down on Engel, on account of he trusted him so much. He don't even want to hear Engel's name, much less to defend him.

Fred: Don't worry, I'll keep my mouth shut. Woops, there's somebody on the other line. I'll be talking to you.

Rapaport: Right. See you, Fred.

Fred hung up, and Engel walked back around to the other side of the desk and said, "You don't have another line."

"Rapaport don't know that."

"I appreciate this, Fred, and now I'm off."

"Al, you understand I got to call Nick as soon as you leave. And I got to tell him you know about Herbert Rose."

"Sure, I know that. You got a phone book?"

"Oh, yeah. Here."

Fred dragged a directory out of a desk drawer, and in it Engel found Herbert Rose with a home address on East 82nd Street, and Rose Cartage Company with an address on West 37th Street, over near the piers. He shut the directory and said, "Well, that's that."

Fred said, "I wish you luck, Al, because I believe you. And you know why I believe you? I believe you because if you were guilty you'd already know what Rose's first name was and where to find him, am I right?"

"Right as rain, Fred." Engel leaned down over the desk, looking in Fred's eyes. "You look tired, Fred," he said, and his right fist came around very fast and clipped Fred on the side of the jaw. Fred's head snapped back and forward, and Fred was asleep.

Engel was sorry he'd had to do it, but it would give him an extra few minutes, and he needed every spare second he could get. He went to the door, opened it and stepped out, said back into the office, "See you, Fred," and shut the door. To Fancy he said, "Fred don't want to be disturbed for a while."

"Yeah," Fancy said, disgruntled. "That's the standing order around here."

Engel hurried down the stairs to the street, and intercepted one of the odd cabs that had wound up this far over from the center of town. "Thirty-seventh Street and Eleventh Avenue," he said.

The cabby made a face. "Don't anybody go to midtown no more? I been over here the last hour and a half."

"What do you want to go to midtown for? Get in that traffic jam?"

The cabby said, "Yeah, I guess you're right. I didn't look at it that way."

They went over 47th Street and down Eleventh Avenue. The cabby had a transistor radio propped up on the dashboard in the left corner, playing rock and roll music. Then, as they rolled down Eleventh Avenue, it played news instead. They reached 37th Street, and as the cabby was making change for a five-dollar bill, the smallest Engel had on him, the radio said *Aloysius Engel* and began giving his description.

The cabby gave him change and a funny look. And another funny look. And a sort of squint.

Engel got out of the cab and walked away down 37th Street, looking for Rose Cartage Company. Behind him, the damn cabby kept looking and squinting, squinting and looking, and all of a sudden drove very fast away from there.

So how much time did he have? Five minutes? Maybe less.

And who'd get there first, the organization or the cops?

Engel hurried into the open garage door of the building labeled Rose Cartage Company, Herbert Rose, Incorporated.

20

"MR. ROSE?" THE TRUCKER pointed a thumb. "Up them stairs over there and through the door at the end."

"Thanks."

Engel hurried. All around him in the big echoing interior of the building men were working in, on and under trucks. None of them paid him any attention as he strode across the concrete floor and up the wooden stairs at the back.

The door at the end said *Private*, which at the moment meant less than nothing to Engel. He pushed open the door, went in, and there was Rose himself, standing behind a long table completely full of pink and white and yellow slips of paper.

Rose looked up, and blinked, and said, "Oh, my God." Then he fainted. He fell on the table, and slid down off it, followed by all those slips of pink and white and yellow paper, and they settled to the floor around him like snow.

"I got no time for that," said Engel. "No time." He looked around, and in the corner there was a water cooler. He went over, grabbed a paper cup, filled it, and emptied it on Rose's face.

Rose came up sputtering and sneezing and coughing and hacking and smacking himself on the chest.

Engel didn't wait for him to stand. Instead, he squatted down in front of him and said, "Rose."

Rose looked at him, through eyes reddened by coughing and sneezing. Comprehension came into them, and he ducked his head down, putting his arms up, crossed over his head to protect himself. "Please," he said, the word muffled by the fact he was talking into his chest. "Please don't."

Engel slapped his forearms. "Look at me, you moron," he said.

Rose peeked at Engel through his arms.

"You got one minute," Engel told him. "One minute to tell me who sent you to frame me. If I don't get the name in one minute, you're a casualty."

"I'll tell," squeaked Rose. "You don't have to threaten me, I'll tell."

"Fine," said Engel.

Cautiously Rose lowered his arms. "I didn't want to do it at all," he said, "but what choice did I have? I even said if they hurt me I'll tell the truth, I'm no hero for somebody else, why should I? A man can be pushed so far only and that's enough."

"You're right. That's enough. Just the name."

Rose made a motion with his hands as though throwing away the whole thing, washing his hands of it, leaving it behind him. "Mrs. Kane," he said. "Murray Kane's widow, she should have burned up with her husband."

"Margo Kane?"

"Didn't I say it?"

"How?" Engel wanted to know. "How'd she get you to do it?"

"I'm a businessman. A businessman is in business only if other businessmen give him business. Murray Kane was a very important and a very vicious man, Mr. Engel, believe me. With his two brothers also in business, with what he had on this one and that one, he wanted from you a little favor you didn't say no. And the wife the same. Do I want half my customers all of a sudden in somebody else's trucks? So me she calls, and half a dozen others the same way, and what choice we got?"

"You were killing me," Engel told him. "You know that, you bastard?"

"I swear I didn't. 'It'll get him fired,' she said. That's all she wanted, she said, was get you fired."

Could it be? Somebody outside the organization, who didn't exactly know the ethics or the values in the organization; it was possibly so. Maybe Mrs. Kane really hadn't wanted any more than to get Engel fired.

As though you could get fired from the organization! If Nick Rovito gave out a pink slip, the color came from blood.

Engel got to his feet. "All right," he said. It was obvious Rose didn't know anything else. The one to see now was Margo Kane.

But even while he was thinking that, it still failed to make sense. Had Margo Kane stolen Charlie Brody? Had Margo Kane killed Merriweather? If so, why, and why? Knowing who—even assuming he had the who absolutely right this time—still didn't tell him a damn thing about why.

Well. Later. This was neither the time nor the place to be reflective. Engel hurried out of the room again, leaving Rose soggy and scared amid the wet scramble of his papers. Engel hurried down the stairs, across the concrete floor, and out to the street, getting there just as two cars squealed to a stop in front of him.

The one on the left was a pink and white Pontiac, and out of it climbed Gittel and Fox.

The one on the right was a green and white patrol car, and out of it climbed two cops.

Engel turned and ran.

Behind him there were shouts of "Hi!" and "Ho!" and "Halt!" It was the beginning of things all over again, with him running from the grief parlor, except that this time the cast of cops was smaller and there was the added element of Gittel and Fox.

At Eleventh Avenue he turned left, at West 38th Street he turned right. Looking over his shoulder, he saw, half a block back and coming strong, one of the cops and Fox. Which meant the other cop was on the patrol-car radio and Gittel was on the nearest phone.

Escaping on foot was no good, he couldn't distance the two directly behind him, and any minute there'd be a whole double army looming up in front of him.

He ran across Tenth Avenue, snarling traffic.

Between Ninth and Tenth there was one of those trucks with the ride on the back. The operator was standing beside the open door of the cab, a line of children was waiting by the curb, a group of children was in the little cars of the ride—these shaped like flying saucers—and the radio was blaring a song of teen-age love. The truck was fire-engine red and explosion-orange and Atlantic Ocean blue and banana-yellow and Central Park green, and had just recently been washed and polished all over. It shone like a *real* flying saucer, that had just landed from Mars.

Engel didn't think twice. He ran up, shoved the owner out of the way, climbed into the cab, remembered to shift it into first, and he and the truck went tearing down the street.

What a getaway! The glittering rainbow of a truck rocking and careening down the street, the children whooping and hollering as their twenty-five-cent ride suddenly began to exceed their wildest dreams, the little flying saucers swooping and circling on the back, the loudspeaker blaring . . . People along the right of way smiled and laughed, little children waved their hands and jumped up and down and in their excitement lost their grip on balloons, shopkeepers trotted out to the sidewalk in their aprons to wave and smile beneath straw hats, the drivers of cars and buses and trucks pulled over and, laughing, waved him through . . .

And then the loudspeaker began to talk. "BE ON THE LOOKOUT," it told the world, "FOR ALOYSIOUS ENGEL, SIX FOOT ONE INCH TALL, WEIGHT—"

21

ENGEL WAS A NERVOUS wreck. He sat in a bar at the end of no-where and shakily raised a glass of Scotch on the rocks to his lips, sipped, and put the glass down again.

He'd finally abandoned that damn truck and its load of delighted kids in the middle of 14th Street, near Eighth Avenue. With the instinct of a hunted animal, he'd then gone to ground, ducking into the first hole he saw, which happened to be the entrance to the subway. He went down flight after flight of concrete stairs flanked by yellow tile walls, and at the very bottom found the dingiest old subway train in the world, sitting down there as though time had stopped along about 1948. It had passengers to match, all sitting there silent and fat and kind of seedy, most of them reading newspapers which must surely have been predicting the election of Thomas E. Dewey. Engel had gotten aboard this train, and the doors had shut behind him, and the train had started off through the dark tunnel, stopping now and again, going under the East River to Brooklyn, eventually coming up for air and riding along as an elevated for a while, coming down to sit like a regular train at ground level by the time it reached the end of the line.

Engel had never ridden this line before. He got off the train when it came to its last stop, and he was still in 1948. Wooden platform. Low buildings all around, old unrich residential, two-family houses. Engel walked to the nearest bar, ordered Scotch on the rocks, and waited for his nerves to settle down.

The bar was named Rockaway Grill. Wasn't there a section of Queens called Far Rockaway? Engel said to the barman, "What section is this?"

"Canarsie."

Canarsie. Engel said, "In Brooklyn?"

"Sure in Brooklyn."

"Good. You got a Manhattan phone book?"

"Yeah. Hold on."

In the phone book Engel found Kane, Murray 198 E 68 ELdrdo 6-9970. "Thanks," he said, and pushed the phone book back across the bar. "Fill the glass again."

"Right."

"A double."

"Right."

Three doubles later he was calm enough to leave the bar, go back to the subway station, and take the next train back to Manhattan. He got out at Union Square, and it was just five o'clock, and everybody had showed up for the rush hour. Since he hadn't eaten since breakfast, and it's impossible to go anywhere at rush hour in New York, and it would be better to wait till after dark before he did any more traveling anyway, he went into a little restaurant on University Place and had himself a meal.

Through all of this, as time continued to tick along, he kept trying to figure it out. It was *possible,* of course, that Margo Kane had done everything, had stolen Charlie and murdered Merriweather and aimed Rose. As for Rose, that was definite, proved, no question. As for Merriweather, there was no doubt she'd been there, but somehow Engel just couldn't see her wielding the knife. Besides, her reaction on seeing the body had been too good to be false. And, for a further besides, what about her crazy you-murdered-my-husband line? He no longer believed the explanation she'd given him for that scene, but he couldn't think of any other explanation to take its place. As for stealing Charlie, there was still the problem of what she could possibly have wanted him for.

Margo Kane. He thought and thought. Margo Kane was linked up one way or another with Kurt Brock. Maybe he was the one who'd asked her to use her contacts to frame Engel. Maybe Brock was the one who'd stolen Charlie's body; he sure had more opportunity than anybody else. Maybe he'd loused up one of the things he was supposed to do, the embalming and all that, and so he hid the body instead of putting it in the casket, but then Merriweather found out about it and Brock had to kill him and—

Aside from being the most stupid idea he'd had all week, that was impossible. Brock had an airtight alibi.

All right. He still didn't have enough information, that's all it was. He'd have to wait till he saw Margo Kane, and when he saw her he'd be damn sure to get the truth out of her.

He was impatient, and finally decided he couldn't wait till after dark. He paid for his meal, all of which he'd eaten but none of which he'd tasted, left the restaurant at five minutes to six, and at ten minutes after six he had a cab, mainly by bumping an old woman with a lot of packages from Klein's out of contention.

"That got her," said the cabby. He didn't care who won, they all had money.

"Third Avenue and 67th Street," Engel told him.

"Check."

The cabby had paid no real attention to his face, and he didn't have a portable radio, so Engel felt relatively safe for the moment. He sat far in the corner of the back seat, directly behind the cabby, and kept his face turned away from the pedestrians outside the window.

The trip uptown was nerve-racking, but it was the driver's nerves that were being racked, not Engel's. He got out at 67th Street, paid and left a tip average enough to assure that the cabby would have no special reason to remember him, and then walked up to 68th Street and headed west.

Number 198 was an old brownstone, with well-tended greenery in its tiny square of yard beside the front steps. The ground-floor windows were barred, and a barred gate closed off the ground-floor entrance beneath the steps. The first floor displayed two extremely tall windows to the left of the main entrance at the head of the steps, and the windows on the second and third floors sported green window boxes. Lights were on behind the first- and second-floor windows.

Engel walked past the house the first time, checking to see if either the cops or the organization people were watching here. So far as he could tell, it was clear. He turned around, walked back, and climbed the steps to the front door.

There were two doorbells, the upper one marked "Wright" and the lower marked "Kane." Engel rang the Kane bell, and waited, and after a minute a grill beside the door said, in a tinny imitation of Margo Kane's voice, "Who is it, please?"

Engel leaned close to the grill. "Engel," he said. He had to play it boldly now. If she refused to let him in, he'd have to get in some other way.

But she said, "One minute, please, Mr. Engel," and less than a minute later she was at the front door, opening it, smiling at him, saying, "You've become a very famous man since I saw you last. Come in, come in."

She was wearing black stretch pants and a black and red striped sweater and red slippers. She seemed as innocent and charming and undangerous as ever.

Engel stepped in and shut the door. "Thanks for letting me in."

"Not at all, not at all. Come along, we'll sit in the living room." As she led the way down a long dark carpeted hall with a chandelier above, she said over her shoulder, "You didn't tell me your gangster business included rubbing people out. That is the phrase, isn't it? Rubbing people out?"

"That's the phrase."

She pushed apart sliding doors and they stepped through into the living room, where the tall windows were. "Sit down anywhere," she said, shutting the sliding doors again behind them.

The room was done in off-white, with Persian throw rugs and expensive antiques all over the place, and the highest ceiling this side of a basketball court. The flooring gleamed, a towering pier glass stretched up between the front windows, and midway in the long wall opposite the double doors there was a marble fireplace containing the ashes of a real fire.

"Something to drink?" she said. "A nice ruby port?"

"Nothing for me." He settled on a Victorian chair that looked rickety but wasn't.

She settled onto an antique davenport nearby. "I suppose," she said, "you came to ask me to give you some sort of alibi for last night, but I'm terribly afraid I can't. Even if the times were right, and they aren't, you know, we *were* back in the city in plenty of time for you to have gone over to New Jersey and killed that poor man, but even if that weren't true I still wouldn't dare admit I spent any part of last night with you in New England. You understand."

"That isn't what I'm here about," Engel said.

"Oh?"

"I'm here to ask you how come you sent Herbert Rose to frame me."

She smiled, rather uncertainly. "Herbert Rose? Did he see you do the shooting or something?"

"Maybe you didn't know what a good frame it was," Engel told her. "Maybe you just thought I'd get into enough trouble to stop me looking for Charlie Brody."

"Charlie—? All these names, Mr. Engel, I'm sorry—"

"That's okay," said Engel. "Don't let it worry you."

"Well, I just wish I knew what you were talking about, that's all."

Engel said, "The story Rose told my boss was enough to make my boss order me rubbed out. That's the phrase, Mrs. Kane, rubbed out."

Her eyes widened. "Oh," she said. "Surely not. Just for stealing?"

"You just made an admission," Engel pointed out.

She brushed it away impatiently. "Of course I did. I was the one who talked to Herbert Rose and the others. I did it last night long-distance from Connecticut."

"While you were at the powder room."

"Of course. And do you know why?"

"You're going to tell me why," Engel said.

"That's right, I am. Because I like you, that's why."

Engel said, "What was that?"

"Forgive me if I give you a swelled head, Mr. Engel, but I must admit I found you a fascinating man. If only, I thought, if only Mr. Engel could get out of that gangster business and into something safer and more acceptable, there's no telling where my feelings for him might go."

Engel watched her with his mouth hanging open. "You're incredible," he said. "You're unbelievable."

"So I thought," she sailed serenely on, "I thought the thing to do was get you in trouble with all the gangsters so they'd throw you out. And *then* I could talk to you, guide you, help you, and the first thing you know—"

"Stop it," said Engel.

"Well, good heavens," she said, "I didn't think they'd be mad enough to *kill* you! Why should they anyway, they're a bunch of crooks themselves, aren't they?"

That much Engel believed, that she hadn't known she was putting a death sentence on him with her little frame. As for the rest, it would wash a lot of hogs. In order to set things straight, therefore, he took a couple minutes out to explain to her just why the frame had been so lethal, and then he took a couple minutes more to explain that the Menchik murder was an additional frame growing out of the first one. "*That's* what you did to me," he said.

"Well, good heavens," she said. "Good heavens. I'm terribly sorry, I really am. I don't know what I can do about the murder, but I can surely set things right with your boss. I'll call Herbert Rose and the others right this minute and tell them to go to your boss and tell him the truth."

Engel pointed. "There's the phone," he said.

"You doubt me?" She got to her feet and went over to the phone and dialed. "Herbert, please," she said, and then a minute later, "Herbert? This *is* Mrs. Kane." Her voice had noticeably harshened. "I'm changing my mind about Mr. Engel. I want you to go back and tell the truth, admit that you lied about Mr. Engel."

Engel went over and took the phone out of her hand and listened. "—beat me up or some such—" It was the voice of Herbert Rose all right. He handed the phone back to her.

She gave him a look that said "smarty pants," and into the phone said, "I don't care about that, Herbert. You tell them the whole truth, except for my name. Don't tell them my name, just say Mr. Engel will explain that part of it. But tell them you were forced to do it and you're sorry. And I'll call the others and tell them the same thing. Yes, I will. You do that right now, Herbert. Yes, Herbert. Good-bye, Herbert."

She made four more phone calls, all of a same order, all equally legitimate, and when she was done she said, "There! All fixed."

"Except for the murder rap."

"Well, your bosses started that, so let them stop it."

"Yeah, sure."

"I've done what I can," she said. She seemed to be pouting now, as though she'd expected him to be more pleased.

"There's still more," Engel said.

"What more could there be?"

"Why'd you steal Charlie Brody? Where is he now? Why'd you kill Merriweather?"

"Steal—kill—*what?*"

"No," said Engel. "*You* didn't do it all, that isn't your style. You send other people to do it for you. Like you sent Rose to take care of me, because he could do it and you couldn't. So I suppose you had Kurt Brock get the—"

"I never heard that name in my—"

"I saw you go in his apartment yesterday afternoon, when he told you I'd been there. That's why you called me to have dinner with you, so you could find out what I was up to."

She seemed really angry now. "I have no idea," she said, "what you're talking about."

"I'd just left him before you got there," Engel said. "I was still out front."

"That's impossible. I would have seen you!"

"You were in too much of a hurry to see Brock!"

"Kurt Brock is nothing to me, nothing. He consoled me in my grief, that's all, I have no connection with him, I don't even know why you bring him up." Now she was distraught, a lace handkerchief being rummaged in her hands. "Why be jealous of him?" she cried. "In comparison with you he's—"

"Stop that!"

"Don't *shout* at me!"

Engel opened his mouth, then shut it and inhaled instead. Then, softly, he said, "All right. I won't shout. I'll just tell you what I know, and when I'm done you tell me the rest."

"I'm beginning," she said, "to get tired of—"

"If you keep interrupting," he said, "I'll have to shout."

She closed her mouth with a snap, and turned her head to glare toward the pier glass.

Engel said, "Your style is send somebody else to do the job. Send Rose to take care of me. Send Kurt to get Charlie Brady's body. Did you kill Merriweather yourself, or did you send somebody else to do that, too? And will you tell me for Christ's sake what you wanted with Charlie Brady's body?"

She jumped to her feet. "What about *you?*" she shrieked. "Charlie Brady's body, Charlie Brady's body, can't you think of anything *else?* You've been driving me crazy, you never stop, what's the use of it? The man's dead, what do you want with his body?"

"What do *you* want with it?"

"Nothing, I don't have it, I don't know what you're—"

"You've got it!" Engel snapped at her. "You didn't get it yourself, you sent somebody else to get it for you, but *you got it!* What do you—?" And he stopped, open-mouthed.

She looked at him. "What?" she said.

"Uh huh," he said. He was looking into the middle distance, but his expression was more as though he were looking inward, watching a movie being screened on the inside of his skull. "Yeah," he said, and nodded. "That'd do it," he said.

"Do what?" She came closer to him, dropping the handkerchief in her distraction. "What are you thinking now?"

"Things going bad," he said. "Spending faster than you earn, you'd do it, that's your style. And stealing from the business, that'd fit in. And probably owe the government back taxes. Everything closing in all at once." He spread his arms around. "You've got a place like this—"

"We rent the top two floors," she said quickly. "That helps with taxes and upkeep. Murray and I just live here and downstairs."

"A Mercedes," he said, "That'd be *your* car, your husband would have a car of his own, a Cadillac . . ."

"Lincoln," she said. "Continental. Cadillac is common."

He nodded. "That's right. Everything goes together nice."

"I wish," she said, "I really wish I knew what you were talking about."

He looked around, and there was another set of closed double doors at the far end of the room. He moved toward them, slowly, saying, "It's easy when you look at it right, put everything together the right way. Like a jigsaw puzzle. Like you always send somebody else to do what you can't do, you do that all the time. So the only question is, what did you send Charlie Brody to do that you couldn't do yourself?"

"You are completely out of your mind. Come away from there."

"And the answer," he said, his hands touching the doors, "is that you sent Charlie Brody to take the place of"—he slid the doors open—"you," he said to the heavy-set glint-eyed man standing there in the darkness.

The heavy-set man smiled, and took a gun from his pocket, and aimed the gun at Engel.

"Murray Kane," said Engel. "You're Murray Kane."

"How do you do, Mr. Engel," said Murray Kane.

Behind Engel, the woman said, "Now see what you've done? You've just made things impossible for yourself."

"My wife is correct, Mr. Engel," said Kane. "You have made things impossible for yourself."

"Insurance," said Engel. He didn't have time yet to think about the mess he was in; he'd just figured things out and he was still involved with fitting all the pieces in place. "You'll be insured to the hilt, and your wife collects. Your debts die with you, and your wife can sell the business. The two of you take off for anywhere, Brazil, Europe—"

"The Caribbean," said Kane.

"And you're set for life."

Kane smiled again. "For death," he said softly. "Set for death."

"So," said Engel, "your wife got close to Kurt Brock—"

Kane's smile soured a trifle. "Perhaps a bit *too* close," he said, and directed his sour smile past Engel to his wife.

"I did what I had to do," she said. "This was your idea, Murray."

"What you had to wait for," said Engel, "was a suitable body, a body loused up some way so there'd be no viewing. Then Brock stole the body, you put it in your factory and set fire to the place, and as far as anybody's concerned Murray Kane is dead."

"As a doornail," said Kane.

"But Merriweather got suspicious somehow."

Kane's smile twisted even more. "He eavesdropped. He overheard Brock and my wife talking. He tried to blackmail us, to cut himself in for a percentage."

Mrs. Kane said, "You were just going to talk to him, that's all. You and your temper."

"He was too greedy," said Kane. "A fool, and too greedy."

Mrs. Kane said, "If we're going to talk, why don't we all sit down?"

"Of course," said Kane. "Mr. Engel, forgive me. I didn't mean to keep you standing. If you will be so good as to walk very slowly to that chair there, and sit down with no sudden or excitable moves, I would be most appreciative."

They all sat down in the living room, at a good distance from one another. Mrs. Kane said, "Now, where were we? Oh, yes. Murray went to see Mr. Merriweather, and I had the most awful premonition, so I followed him. I knew poor Kurt had been fired, for nuzzling with me behind the flowers, and when I saw you standing in the office, Mr. Engel, from behind, I thought you were Kurt, and I was terribly afraid you'd see Murray. You see, Kurt doesn't know my husband's alive."

Murray smiled again. "Kurt understands an entirely different plot," he said, "culminating in his running off to Hawaii with Margo and half a million dollars."

"Poor Kurt," said Mrs. Kane. "He'll be so disappointed. At any rate, I saw you and thought you were Kurt, and so I said, 'What are you doing here?' because of course I knew you'd been fired. Then you turned around, and you weren't Kurt, and Mr. Merriweather was dead, and it was too much for me, so I fainted."

Murray said, "My wife faints whenever things are too much for her, Mr. Engel."

"Then I woke up," said Mrs. Kane, "and Murray was there. He'd been hiding on the cellar staircase. Well, the building was just full of policemen, so what was I to do?"

Engel said, "You sicked them on me."

"Just so Murray could get away. Then things began to get complicated. I kept having to see you, to find out what you were doing, whether you were dangerous to us or not. And finally I had to get you in trouble with your boss, though I truly didn't mean you to get in as much trouble as you did."

The husband said, "You should have let well enough alone, Engel. My wife went to the trouble of calling Rose and the others back, fixing things up for you again. You should have quit while you were ahead."

"I still had my job to do," Engel said.

Mrs. Kane got to her feet and said, "All right, now we've told you everything. Now will you, for the love of God, tell *me* something?"

"You? Sure, what?"

"What are you up to, Mr. Engel? What do you keep snooping around for?"

"Charlie Brody. I was sent to get his body back."

"But *why?* How did you even know he was missing?"

"I dug up his coffin and he wasn't in it."

The Kanes looked at each other. Mrs. Kane said, "Mr. Engel, I've got to know why. What set you off?"

"Charlie's suit," Engel said.

"His suit?"

"There was something in it my boss wanted."

They looked at each other again. Mrs. Kane said, "The suit. All the time, it wasn't the body at all, it was the suit."

"We wanted the body suitable," said Kane, "and he wanted the body's suit."

Engel said, "What did you do with it?"

Mrs. Kane shrugged. "I have no idea. Kurt took care of all that. I gave him one of Murray's suits to dress it in."

"So Kurt would know where the suit is."

Kane said, "You understand, Mr. Engel, so far as you are concerned all this has become academic. It won't be possible to let you live."

Mrs. Kane said, "Murray, I don't like this at all. At first it was just a simple honest insurance swindle, but now it's becoming criminal. You've already murdered one man in cold blood, and now you're going to do it again. Murray, you can't allow yourself to get into the habit of thinking of murder as the solution to all your problems."

"Don't you lecture me," Kane snapped. Then he composed his face again in the lines of pleasant humor, and said to Engel, "I'm sorry, Mr. Engel, I truly am. But I don't dare leave anyone who knows I'm still alive."

"Sure," said Engel. He was thinking. Jump through one of the tall windows? He'd never get there in time. No, wait and see what developed.

Mrs. Kane was saying, "But how, Murray? What are we going to do with *his* body?" Abruptly, she giggled. "All at once we've got more bodies than we know what to do with."

"Oh, I know what to do with Mr. Engel," Kane said. "Yes, indeed. Mr. Engel won't be found, darling, don't you worry your pretty head about it."

"You know what to do with him?"

"That I do."

"What? Tell me!"

"I know a grave," quoth Kane, "without a body. A casket and all, but no body." He smiled upon Engel. "You won't mind too awfully much, Mr. Engel," he said, "if your headstone should read *Brody?*"

22

THE NICE THING ABOUT the trunk of a Lincoln Continental, it's roomy. The bad thing about this particular Lincoln Continental was that Engel had to share it with a spade, a pick, a flashlight, a jack, a set of tire chains, and something small and round and cold and hard that kept sticking him in the small of the back.

The condition of the streets of New York City are a disgrace, a real disgrace. Back around 1960 the city hired some men to go out and paint yellow lines around all the potholes for some reason, but other than that and since then the potholes have been left to themselves. Engel, riding to and across Brooklyn in the trunk of Kane's car, devoted a number of thoughts to the municipal government of the City of New York.

But all good things come to an end, and with a final jounce this ride did too. Engel waited, gripping the jack handle in the dark inside the trunk, thinking there was just a chance he'd be able to knock the gun out of Murray Kane's hand as the trunk lid was being raised.

But no such luck. It was Margo Kane who opened the trunk, while her husband stood well back and slightly to one side, where Engel couldn't get at him but Margo didn't block her husband's aim.

"Leave the jack there, Engel," Kane said. "But do bring the pick and shovel and flashlight. Margo, get the blanket from the back seat."

It was the well-remembered path to the well-remembered grave, except that last time Willy Menchik had been along. Yes, and last time it was Willy Menchik who had been slated to go into the grave. Things were a bit different now.

It was still early, only a little past nine, but the cemetery was as deserted as if it were three o'clock in the morning. They clinked and tinkled along the path to the still-raw grave, Margo spread the blanket for a groundcloth, and for the second time in three days Engel proceeded to dig up Charlie Brody's grave.

The job seemed to go quicker this time, probably because last time he was in a hurry to be done and this time he was in no hurry at all, and so both times ran wrong, with the usual perversity of life. In just minutes Engel was down to the coffin, his spade making a hollow sound as it hit the top of the box.

Kane came over, saying, "Is that it?"

"That's it."

"Open it."

"I can't while I'm standing on it. I had this trouble last time, and I had to get out to do it."

Kane made an impatient gesture. "Then come up out of there."

Engel's gesture signified helplessness. "I'll need a pull."

Kane cocked his head to one side. "Is that so? Think to pull me in with you, wrest the gun away, get the upper hand, is that it? Margo."

She came forward.

Kane handed her the gun. "Cover him. If he even starts to act up, shoot."

"All right, Murray," she said, but she sounded doubtful. "It's awful damn spooky here," she said.

"It didn't bother you up to now," he said.

"Oh, Murray," she said, and abruptly fainted, dropping the gun into the grave, where it bounced on the coffin.

Engel had it in his hand before it could bounce twice, and had it trained on Murray Kane, who was poised in indecision, not quite in flight away from here and not quite diving on top of Engel. "Easy," Engel said. "Take it easy, Kane."

"Engel, I can make it worth your—"

"Don't waste your breath, Kane. I'm not going to kill you. Why should I?"

Kane gaped at him. On the ground his wife moaned.

Engel said, "Don't you get it? The faint was an act, a gamble. Either I got the gun and killed you, or you got the gun and killed me. She didn't care which way it went. If you killed me, she'd have to figure another way to take care of you later."

"What's that?"

"It's Brock she wants, not you. She doesn't need you around to inherit." Engel hefted the gun. "And this is her style, you got to admit it. This time, she sent *me* to do the job."

Kane started to growl.

Margo Kane sat up, being bewildered and semi-conscious. "What—what happened?"

"You conniving bitch!" shouted Kane.

Margo hesitated, then flashed Engel a look of cold hate. "I won't forget you!"

"It's mutual, honey," said Engel.

Kane had grabbed the pick, and was now advancing around the grave toward his wife. "You'll pay," he was growling, "this time you'll pay, you—" And so on.

She saw him coming, and scrambled to her feet. With a roar he came running around the grave, and with a yelp she fled into the darkness. Shouting, shrieking, bellowing, screaming, crashing around, the Kanes careened away across the tombstoned landscape, out of sight and—a minute or two later—out of hearing.

Engel stuck the gun in his pocket and clambered out of the grave. He didn't have either the patience or the inclination to fill it in yet again, so he just left it there.

The key was in the ignition of the Continental, a car which did not, needless to say, have a standard shift. In addition, its front seat offered a much gentler and smoother ride than did its trunk. The trip back across Brooklyn was smooth as silk.

A little after ten, on West 24th Street, Engel parked in front of the same fire hydrant Margo Kane had parked her Mercedes in front of yesterday. He crossed the street, rang Kurt Brock's bell, and was rewarded by a buzzing sound which meant he could push open the downstairs door now.

Brock was standing in his doorway upstairs. "You," he said. "You told me you were a policeman." He seemed indignant.

"You're lucky I'm not," Engel told him. "It's against the law to steal dead bodies. It's a misdemeanor." Engel pushed him back from the doorway, stepped in, and shut the door. "You could get thirty days," he said.

"What? What? I don't know what—"

"I'm talking about. Yeah, I know, I've heard that line before tonight." Engel took out the gun, held it casually in his palm, and said, "Where do you suppose I got this? Guess who I got it from. Go on, guess."

Brock was staring at the gun. "What are you, what are you going to—?"

"I won't use it on you, don't worry. Not unless I have to. You can't guess where I got it? Then I'll have to tell you. From Murray Kane."

"Murr—Murr—"

"Yeah. Murray Kane. What kind of song and dance did his wife give you, anyway? What did you think that body was for?"

"I—I really—please, I don't—"

"Cut it out, Brock. The stiff's name was Charles Brody. Burned face, no viewing."

Brock was shaking his head, back and forth, back and forth, very monotonously.

Engel said, "Brody was buried today in a grave marked Murray Kane. Where did you think Murray was? He's alive, you know."

"No," whispered Brock, still doing that metronome thing with his head, "no, he isn't. He drowned."

"Drowned? Oh, is that what she told you?" Engel laughed. "She's good, Margo is. I can hear the spiel now. She's killed Murray because she loves you, but his body's at the bottom of the lake and there's no way to prove he's dead, so the inheritance will be tied up and all, so the thing to do is get another body and fix it so it'll look like Murray and arrange for Murray to die all over again."

"How did you—?"

"Because Murray's alive. It was the insurance swindle. Margo double-crossed you."

"No, she wouldn't. She wouldn't."

"You're running away to Hawaii together."

"Yes!"

"She told me that's what you thought."

"Thought?" The truth, all at once, was beginning to seep into Brock. "*Thought?* She never meant to—She wasn't going to—"

"Not for a minute."

"Where—?"

"I don't know exactly. The last I saw her, Murray was chasing her through a cemetery with a pick in his hands. But she's pretty fast, she might get away from him. If she does, she might come here, but if I were you I wouldn't let her in. Murray's liable to come here too, looking for her, and it probably wouldn't be smart to let him in either."

"Murray . . ."

"Murray thinks his wife went a bit overboard getting your co-operation."

Brock automatically glanced toward the zebra-stripe couch, and licked his lips nervously. "I got to get out of here," he said. "I got to clear out before they get here."

Engel stood blocking the door. "One small thing," he said, "and then you can go."

"No, really, I got to—"

"One question," Engel told him. "Stand still a second and listen to me. One question, and then you can take off wherever you want."

Brock controlled himself with an obvious effort. "What? I'll tell you, anything you want, what is it?"

"The suit," Engel said.

"Suit?"

"Brody was wearing a suit," Engel said. "A blue suit."

Brock shook his head. "No, he wasn't."

"What?"

"He was wearing a brown suit."

"A brown suit."

"Sure. I cremated it."

"You did what?"

"Mr. Merriweather had his own crematorium out back, and I burned it up in there. It might have been evidence."

"And it was a brown suit, not a blue suit. A brown suit, you're sure of that."

"Oh, yes. I noticed he had on a brown suit and black shoes. You're not supposed to do that, you know."

"Yeah, that's right."

"Can I go now?"

Engel grinned at him. "Yeah," he said. "You can go."

"I don't know what you want with Brody's suit," Brock said earnestly, "but I can guarantee the suit he wore at Mr. Merri-weather's was brown."

"I believe you," Engel told him. "Oh, I believe you."

Brock headed for the door, and Engel said, "One thing more."

"Now what?"

"If anybody else ever asks you about that suit, you tell them it was the blue one and you burned it. You got that? The blue one, and you burned it. If you say that, you won't get into any trouble."

"Then I'll say it," Brock promised.

"Good," said Engel, and laughed out loud.

He followed Brock downstairs to the street, chuckling and shaking his head.

23

ONCE AGAIN HE WENT down the fire escape and through the window and across the black bedroom to the light switch, but this time when he turned on the light he remained alone.

He hadn't expected to find her here, and he was right. She was gone, taking nothing with her. On the kitchen table, where he'd left his note, there was a new note in its place. It read:

Dear Mister Engel,

I don't know if you will ever get this note but if you do I want you to know I appreciate everything you have done for me and the memory of my former husband Charles Brody.

I have gone away as I guess by now you know why and intend to begin a new life for myself somewhere very far away. A girl does not get any younger and I really did not feel it best for me to go back to work for Archie Freihofer after all.

I have ironed your underwear and left it for you on the living room sofa.

Very sincerely yours,
Bobbi Bounds Brody

It was there all right, clean and glimmering and without a wrinkle. The socks were even rolled in a ball.

That girl, Engel reflected, was going to make some guy in some far-off clime a hell of a wife. Cook and wash and sew for him, take care of him just fine in the bedroom, devote herself to him day and night. And what a dowry: a quarter of a million bucks in uncut heroin!

"She deserves to keep it," Engel told himself aloud, "and Nick Rovito, that faithless friend, deserves not to get it."

He went over to the phone and dialed Nick Rovito's home number, and pretty soon Nick Rovito himself came on the line, saying, "All You okay, boy?"

"I'm fine, Nick. You heard from Rose and the other guys?"

"They'll pay, Al, I guarantee you they'll pay."

"Why? They were muscled into it. You can't down a guy for doing something when he was muscled into it."

"Al, boy, you got a heart as big as all outdoors, you know that, kid? To forgive like that, that's a magnificent gesture."

"Yeah, well . . ."

"Rose tells me I'll get the rest of the story from you."

"Yeah. A woman named Margo Kane hijacked Charlie's body in order to . . ." And for the next five minutes Engel told the full story, leaving out only the final discovery about the blue suit. When he was done, Nick Rovito said, "Well, that's the way it goes. Burned up, huh?"

"Cremated. Nothing left but ashes."

"That disappoints me, but it could be worse. I could of not found out the truth about you, huh, kid? I could of gone on thinking you were disloyal and a bastard. I'm happy to have it straightened out, kid. It's worth the loss of the snow to have you back."

"What about the Menchik frame?"

"Squared. Done tonight, within the last hour. We worked hard, kid, believe me we did. And cost? An arm and a leg. You know, it cost just as much as if you'd been guilty!" And Nick Rovito laughed.

Engel said, "That's good. So I'm in the clear."

"Right. Take a week off, a couple weeks, then come in, we'll—"

"No, Nick."

"What's that?"

"Not after what's happened, Nick. I don't work for you any more."

"Kid, I squared it, it's all square."

"Not with me, Nick. We're quits. No hard feelings, but I just don't want to work for you any more."

Suspicion in his voice, Nick Rovito said, "You got an offer from somebody else? Winocki in Chicago?"

"Nobody else, Nick."

"Let me tell you something. You say you want to quit, okay, quit. But all the way, kid. If you quit, it means out of the organization all the way. I send your name down to the Committee, nobody should ever hire you. Nobody's out for you, but nobody hires you."

"That's okay, Nick. I want to stay out of the organization anyway."

"Well, I think you're crazy. You got a great future with the organization. Some day you could be one of the guys on the Committee yourself."

"No, Nick."

"Have it your own way," Nick Rovito said grumpily, and hung up.

Engel gathered up his underwear and went home.

24

THERE WAS A NOTE on the door, stuck on as usual with a false fingernail, and written so belligerently with flame-red lipstick that the words were just barely legible. It read, more or less:

> All right for you,
> you *rat*!
> I'm going back
> to Cal.
> Good-bye, you
> BASTARD!!!!!

Again there was no signature, and again none was needed.

Engel plucked the note from the door, unlocked the door and went on into the apartment. He shut the door, crossed the foyer, entered the living room, and found Callaghan sitting on the white leather sofa. He was in civvies, and it was amazing how much he looked like Jimmy Gleason on a bad day.

Engel said, "Didn't you get the word? I'm clean."

"Like you were washed with Brand X," said Callaghan. He pushed himself to his feet. "That wasn't my jurisdiction anyway," he said. "You worked that little miscarriage of justice over in Jersey."

"Let's put it this way," said Engel. "It was a frame."

"It always is," said Callaghan.

"This time it was. Think about it, wasn't it too neat? And wasn't it too easy? If I'm nothing else, I'm anyway a professional."

Callaghan frowned. "The thought had crossed my mind," he said. "But I wouldn't look a gift horse in the mouth. If I could get you, Engel, I wouldn't care if it was a frame or not."

Engel shook his head. "You're an honest cop," he said. "You wouldn't do that."

Callaghan turned away and rubbed his hand across his face. "You smart boys," he said.

"I'm out of the rackets," Engel told him.

"Sure you are."

"On the level. I quit Nick tonight. Because of the frame, and some other things. He didn't give me a square deal."

Callaghan studied him a minute and then said, "You know what? I don't care about that for a minute. I came here to tell you something, and it don't matter to me who you work for, what I got to say still applies."

"Go ahead."

"I'm after you, Engel. If you're smart, you'll get out of New York till you hear I'm retired or dead, because I'm out to get you. I got a very small, a very select list of names, and you just joined it."

"How are the other guys on the list doing?"

"Most of them died in the chair, Engel. A few of them I go up the river to Sing Sing and pay them a visit every once in a while. The only reason I pay any attention to a punk like you is the list is getting so short these days." Callaghan picked up a battered civilian hat from the sofa. "I'll be seeing you around, Engel," he said.

'Yeah," said Engel. "Sure."

Callaghan left, and Engel made himself a drink to calm his nerves. After everything was settled, to have Callaghan still breathing down his neck was less than cheery news.

The phone rang. He went over and picked it up and heard, "Aloysius, I've been calling and calling and—"

"California," said Engel.

"Now, you just stop that. I don't want to hear another word about California. What I want to know is, are you coming to dinner tomorrow night or aren't you? I'm only your mother, but—"

"That's it," said Engel. "Good-bye forever." He hung up, strode to the bedroom, and packed two bags while the phone rang. After a while the bags were all packed and the phone had stopped ringing, so he picked it up and called Dolly's friend Roxanne to find out what Dolly's California address was. Roxanne told him, and then said, "Boy, Al, she was sore at you. You should of called or something."

"Yeah," said Engel. "I was kind of busy. But that's all over now."

About the Author

Donald E. Westlake (1933–2008) was one of the most prolific and talented authors of American crime fiction. He began his career in the late 1950s, churning out novels for pulp houses—often writing as many as four novels a year under various pseudonyms—but soon began publishing under his own name. His most well-known characters were John Dortmunder, an unlucky thief, and a ruthless criminal named Parker. His writing earned him three Edgars and a Grand Master Award from the Mystery Writers of America.

Westlake's cinematic prose and brisk dialogue made his novels attractive to Hollywood, and several motion pictures were made from his books, with stars such as Lee Marvin and Mel Gibson. Westlake wrote several screenplays himself, receiving an Academy Award nomination for his adaptation of *The Grifters*, Jim Thompson's noir classic.

DONALD E. WESTLAKE

FROM MYSTERIOUSPRESS.COM
AND OPEN ROAD MEDIA

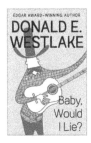

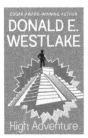

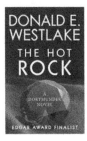
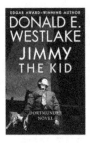
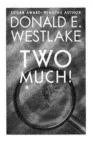

MYSTERIOUSPRESS.COM

Otto Penzler, owner of the Mysterious Bookshop in Manhattan, founded the Mysterious Press in 1975. Penzler quickly became known for his outstanding selection of mystery, crime, and suspense books, both from his imprint and in his store. The imprint was devoted to printing the best books in these genres, using fine paper and top dust-jacket artists, as well as offering many limited, signed editions.

Now the Mysterious Press has gone digital, publishing ebooks through **MysteriousPress.com**.

MysteriousPress.com offers readers essential noir and suspense fiction, hard-boiled crime novels, and the latest thrillers from both debut authors and mystery masters. Discover classics and new voices, all from one legendary source.

FIND OUT MORE AT
WWW.MYSTERIOUSPRESS.COM

FOLLOW US:

@emysteries and Facebook.com/MysteriousPressCom

MysteriousPress.com is one of a select group of publishing partners of Open Road Integrated Media, Inc.

THE MYSTERIOUS BOOKSHOP, founded in 1979, is located in Manhattan's Tribeca neighborhood. It is the oldest and largest mystery-specialty bookstore in America.

The shop stocks the finest selection of new mystery hardcovers, paperbacks, and periodicals. It also features a superb collection of signed modern first editions, rare and collectable works, and Sherlock Holmes titles. The bookshop issues a free monthly newsletter highlighting its book clubs, new releases, events, and recently acquired books.

58 Warren Street
info@mysteriousbookshop.com
(212) 587-1011
Monday through Saturday
11:00 a.m. to 7:00 p.m.

FIND OUT MORE AT:

www.mysteriousbookshop.com

FOLLOW US:

@TheMysterious and Facebook.com/MysteriousBookshop

OPEN ROAD

INTEGRATED MEDIA

Find a full list of our authors and
titles at www.openroadmedia.com

FOLLOW US
@OpenRoadMedia

Printed in the USA
CPSIA information can be obtained
at www.ICGtesting.com
LVHW090757230424
778148LV00001B/43